"How abo[ut] minutes [until] ready?" Nathan asked the boy.

For once Zach didn't argue. But instead of folding himself into his mother's embrace, he lifted his arms to Nathan. "Will you carry me?"

Taken aback, Nathan checked with Catherine again.

"If you don't mind," Catherine said.

He swallowed past the lump in his throat. "I don't mind in the least."

Wrapping his arms around Zach, he hoisted the boy onto his hip and stood, then extended a hand to Catherine.

She accepted his hand and rose. "Let me show you to Zach's room."

The little boy shifted in his arms, emitting a soft sigh, and nestled closer to his heart. Nathan's throat constricted as he stroked a comforting hand over his back. In his whole life he'd never held a child. But the boy felt right in his arms. And good.

Books by Irene Hannon

Steeple Hill Love Inspired

*Home for the Holidays
*A Groom of Her Own
*A Family to Call Her Own
It Had to Be You
One Special Christmas
The Way Home
Never Say Goodbye
Crossroads
**The Best Gift
**Gift from the Heart

*Vows
**Sisters & Brides
†Heartland Homecomings
††Lighthouse Lane

**The Unexpected Gift
All Our Tomorrows
The Family Man
Rainbow's End
†From This Day Forward
†A Dream to Share
†Where Love Abides
Apprentice Father
††Tides of Hope
††The Hero Next Door
††The Doctor's
    Perfect Match
††A Father for Zach

IRENE HANNON

Irene Hannon, who writes both romance and romantic suspense, is the bestselling author of more than thirty novels. Her books have been honored with a coveted RITA® Award from Romance Writers of America (the "Oscar" of romantic fiction), a HOLT Medallion and a Reviewer's Choice Award from *RT Book Reviews*.

A former corporate communications executive with a Fortune 500 company, Irene now writes full-time. In her spare time she enjoys singing, traveling, long walks, cooking, gardening and spending time with family. She and her husband make their home in Missouri.

For more information about her and her books, Irene you to visit her Web site at www.irenehannon.co

A Father for Zach
Irene Hannon

Steeple
Hill®

Published by Steeple Hill Books™

STEEPLE HILL BOOKS

Steeple
Hill®

Recycling programs
for this product may
not exist in your area.

ISBN-13: 978-0-373-81469-5

A FATHER FOR ZACH

Copyright © 2010 by Irene Hannon

www.SteepleHill.com

Printed in U.S.A.

Faith is the realization of what is hoped for and evidence of things not seen.
—*Hebrews* 11:1

To my mom, Dorothy Hannon—and our special memories of Nantucket.

Chapter One

Nathan Clay gazed out over the sparkling blue waters off Nantucket, scanned the pristine white beach and took a long, slow breath.

What a change from the tiny, windowless cell he'd left behind four days ago—his home for the past ten long years.

The juxtaposition was surreal.

Settling back in the white folding chair, he tugged at his unaccustomed tie, surveyed the seventy-five wedding guests assembled on the lush, garden-rimmed lawn that abutted the beach, and tried not to feel out of place. But it was a losing battle. He doubted anyone else in this high-class group had served time in prison. Especially the Supreme Court justice on the other side of the aisle, who was a longtime friend of the Morgan family.

The family his sister, Marci, would be marrying into in just a few minutes.

Talk about moving up in the world.

She deserved it, though. Marci had worked hard to build a better life. To rise above their tough upbringing.

He wished he could have done as well.

Then again, his childhood had been even rougher than Marci's or his big brother's had been. Thanks to the secret that had darkened his life for more years than he cared to recall.

Bile rose in his throat, and he forced himself to swallow past it, to suppress the ugly memories. Those days were history. They couldn't hurt him unless he let them. And he'd resolved never again to give his past that kind of power.

A string quartet positioned to his right began to play, and he focused on the baroque music, letting its measured cadence calm him. Attired in black dresses, the four musicians blended together perfectly, each handling her instrument with a confidence that spoke of long hours of practice.

But it was the violinist who caught his attention. Eyes closed, she swayed slightly as she drew the bow back and forth over the strings, producing pure, clear notes that quivered with emotion.

Nathan didn't know a lot about music. He hadn't had much opportunity to learn to appreciate the finer things in life. But he understood the creative process. Knew all about losing oneself in one's art. That had been his salvation during his decade behind bars. And he sensed this woman felt the same way.

He studied her, appreciating the sweep of her long lashes as they feathered into a graceful arc beneath her eyes. Although her light brown hair was secured at her nape with a barrette, the no-nonsense style was softened by wispy bangs that brushed her smooth brow. The early afternoon sun highlighted her classic bone structure and warmed her flawless complexion, while the whisper of a smile touched her soft, beguiling lips.

Nathan's gaze lingered on their supple fullness…and all at once he found it difficult to breathe.

Reaching up, he ran a finger around his suddenly too-tight collar and forced himself to turn away. Only to discover his new landlady, Edith Shaw, observing him with a smile of her own from two rows back. He had no idea how to interpret the gleam in her eye…nor the wink she directed his way.

And he didn't have a chance to figure it out, because all at once the music changed and an expectant hush fell over the guests.

The minister, groom and best man took their

places beside the wooden gazebo where the vows would be exchanged. Nathan watched his sister-in-law, Heather, start down the aisle. The matron of honor was as radiant as a bride herself—due to the slight bulge in her tummy that heralded the arrival of a new generation of Clays, Nathan suspected.

As the music changed again and Marci appeared on J.C.'s arm, Nathan's breath once more caught in his throat. With her blond tresses and pinup figure, Marci had always been beautiful. But today she was luminous as she slowly made her way toward the gazebo—and the man she would soon promise to love and cherish all the days of her life.

She smiled at him as she approached, her wispy veil drifting behind her in the soft May breeze, her hand tucked in J.C.'s. It was fitting their older brother should walk her down the aisle, Nathan thought. He'd stood by both of them through the tough times, believing in them when neither had believed in themselves.

Much to his surprise, Marci paused beside his chair and reached out to take his hand. "I'm glad you're here, Nathan."

At her soft words, he blinked away the moisture that pooled in his eyes. "So am I."

With a gentle squeeze, she moved on to take her place beside the tall physician who had claimed her heart. As they joined hands beneath swags of white tulle held in place by sprays of pale pink roses and feathery fern, Nathan was glad she'd found her happily-ever-after.

He hoped someday he could do the same.

His escort duties finished, J.C. joined him in the first row. As Nathan shifted over to give his older brother a bit more room, he checked out the violinist again. She was looking over her shoulder now, giving him an excellent view of her appealing profile. Leaning back slightly, Nathan caught a glimpse of a little blond-haired boy sitting behind her on a white folding chair. Her son?

Checking out her left hand, he noted the glint of gold in the early afternoon sun. It figured. She appeared to be in her thirties, and most women that age were married.

Not that it mattered.

The odds of connecting with the first woman to catch his eye were miniscule at best.

But maybe…just maybe…there was a woman out there somewhere who would be able to overlook his past. Who would delve into his heart and see that it had been transformed.

"I, Marci, take you, Christopher…"

As his sister's words echoed strong and sure in the still air, Nathan shifted his attention to the weathered gazebo. Marci stood framed in the lattice archway, her head tipped back, her gaze on the man she loved as she repeated the words after the minister.

Today she would begin a new life.

And so would he, Nathan vowed.

So would he.

An hour later, a piece of cake in one hand and a glass of punch in the other, Nathan stepped into the garden of The Devon Rose. He wasn't surprised Marci and Christopher had decided to have their reception at Heather's tearoom, Lighthouse Lane's most prestigious address. It was where fate—or perhaps the Lord—had brought them together for the second time, setting things in motion for their courtship.

Once more, the genteel music of a string quartet drew his attention. Weaving through the crowd, he followed one of the brick paths that crisscrossed the formal garden with geometric precision.

When the ensemble came into view, he stepped off to one side. It was the same group that had played at the wedding, he noted, homing in on the slender violinist. The musicians must have packed up their instruments and headed straight for the reception the instant the ceremony ended.

The little blond boy was here, too, tucked into a nook a few feet away from his mom, who was shooting him frequent, protective glances. He was sitting on a folding chair, swinging his dangling feet, not in the least interested in the book lying in his lap. Instead, he was hungrily eyeing the plates of cake being juggled by the guests who were milling about.

On impulse, Nathan worked his way through the crowd and headed for the child. Holding out his untouched plate, he smiled. "Would you like some cake?"

The little boy's eyes lit up, but he hesitated and cast a silent plea toward his mother.

As Nathan glanced her way, his stomach knotted at the mistrust in her eyes. He was used to suspicious looks. They'd been part of his life for as long as he could remember. But he'd hoped he'd left them behind.

Summoning up a stiff smile, he waited for her decision.

Finally, without missing a beat of music, she gave a slight nod.

"Oh, boy!"

At the youngster's enthusiastic reaction, Nathan's taut smile softened and he handed over the plate. "How come I knew you liked cake?"

The boy dived in, spearing a hunk of frosting with the fork. "I like the icing best." He proved it by putting the whole glob in his mouth at once. "Than koo."

Chuckling at the garbled expression of gratitude, Nathan lifted his cup of punch in salute. "Well, enjoy it."

He started to walk away, but the boy's voice brought him to a halt. "My name's Zach. What's yours?"

A quick look confirmed that the violinist's jade-green irises were fixed on him. Watchful. Warning him off. Her tense posture was in direct contrast to the soothing classical music emanating from her violin.

Instead of moving back toward the boy, Nathan responded from where he stood. "Nathan."

"You want to see my book?" Zach held up a Dr. Seuss classic, his expression hopeful.

"I don't think your mommy would like that."

Zach's face fell and he lowered the book to his lap. "Yeah. I guess not." He poked at his cake. "The only good thing about weddings is the cake."

"Do you go to a lot of weddings?"

"Uh-huh. They're all the same. Boring."

In his peripheral vision, Nathan could sense the boy's mother still watching him. He wanted to ask Zach some more questions. Find out why he wasn't home with his father. Or a babysitter. Sitting still for such an extended period had to be torture for a youngster.

But he didn't think the woman would appreciate his interest. Not in light of the strong back-off vibes she was sending.

It couldn't be personal, though, he consoled himself. He'd noticed her protective behavior at the wedding, too. And here, as well, even before he'd spoken to Zach. She was just wary, period.

And that raised more questions.

None of which were likely to be answered, Nathan conceded.

Writing off the encounter, he smiled once more at Zach. "Hang in there, champ. It'll be over before you know it."

"That's what Mom always says." The youngster heaved a resigned sigh and continued to shovel the cake into his mouth.

"She's right. It will still be daytime when this party is over. Maybe you can play with your friends later."

"I don't have any friends."

Before Nathan could follow up on that unexpected response, the song ended and the little boy's mother spoke in a soft but insistent voice.

"Zach, come over here and let me wipe that sticky icing off your fingers or it will get all over your jacket."

The youngster speared the last bite of cake and shoved it into his mouth. Scooting off his chair, he trotted over to Nathan and handed him the empty plate. "Thanks a lot. That was good."

"You're welcome."

He took the plate and watched the boy join his mother, she gave him another suspicious scan as she fished a tissue out of her purse and pulled her son close.

Taking the hint, he turned away and strolled back into the crowd of guests. Still wondering why the precocious little blond-haired boy had no friends.

And why the green-eyed beauty was so wary.

"Mom! You're gonna rub all the skin off my face!"

At Zach's protest, Catherine Walker eased off on the vigorous scrubbing she was giving her son's cheeks and double-checked to confirm that the tall, brown-haired man with the slightly gaunt face had disappeared into the throng of wedding guests.

"Sorry, honey." She took one more swipe at a stubborn speck of icing that had somehow found its way to his eyebrow, then pocketed the sticky tissue.

"How much longer is this thing gonna last?"

"A while."

He huffed out a sigh. "That means a really long time."

"I brought a lot of books for you. And there are paper and crayons in the tote bag, too. Why don't you draw some pictures?"

"I'd rather go to the beach."

"I know. We'll go tomorrow, okay?"

"Yeah. I guess." He stuck his hands into his pockets and surveyed the wedding guests. "Maybe that man will come back and talk to me again."

"You know the rule about talking to strangers, Zach."

"He gave me cake. And he was really nice. Besides, he's not a stranger. He told me his name."

"Just because you know his name doesn't mean he's not a stranger."

"You were right here, Mom. You could see me the whole time." Zach gave her a disgruntled look and scuffed the toe of his shoe on the brick walkway. "I wish you weren't so scared all the time."

Jolted, Catherine frowned at him. "I'm not scared. I'm just being cautious."

"What's the difference?"

He wandered back to his seat and began to poke through the tote bag, his apathy for her time-killing suggestions obvious.

As her son withdrew a book and settled into his chair, Catherine pondered his question. What *was* the difference between caution and fear? Not much, she conceded. But she had good reason for both. Thanks to David.

Her stomach clenched, and she forced herself

to take several deep, calming breaths. Someday…maybe…she'd be able to think about him with joy instead of sorrow. But she wasn't there yet. And after two years, she was beginning to wonder if she ever would be.

As for Zach…she was sorry he was unhappy. And she sympathized with his plight. Being confined to a chair for an extended period was about the worst possible punishment you could inflict on a boy his age. In the past, David had watched him during her musical engagements, saving her son this agony. But David was gone. And she didn't trust Zach with anyone else.

Nor had passing up this job been an option. In her short time on Nantucket, the high cost of living had been an unwelcome surprise. She needed the money this gig would bring in.

At a signal from the group's leader, the string quartet struck up "Ode to Joy." Scanning the crowd again, Catherine saw no sign of the man who'd spoken to Zach. That was good. Her trust level with strangers was zilch. Even ones who were guests at a lovely wedding like this. Because you never knew where danger lurked. Sometimes it was found in the most innocent of places. Places you'd assumed were safe.

Yet…as an image of the cake-bearing stranger who'd befriended Zach flashed across her mind, she found it hard to believe he was a man to be feared. Particularly in light of that moment when their gazes had connected. She knew hers had been filled with suspicion, and she wouldn't have been surprised if he'd reciprocated with coolness or antipathy. In fact, that kind of reaction would have been okay.

Instead, she'd been jarred by the hurt in his deep-brown eyes.

All she'd meant to do was warn him off. She hadn't intended to cause him pain. Yet she had. And that disturbed her. A lot. Causing pain was as unacceptable to her as letting Zach out of her sight.

But it was too late to fix things now. She doubted he'd come anywhere close to them again today, considering the unfriendly reception she'd given his kind gesture. And there was little chance their paths would ever cross again.

She needed to let it go.

Catherine tried hard to follow her own advice, doing her best to immerse herself in the lilting, joy-filled strains of one of Beethoven's most uplifting works. To focus on the happy faces of the guests enjoying a perfect celebration in a beautiful garden on this sunny, warm day.

But somehow she couldn't erase the image of a weary face that she sensed belonged to a man who had endured more than his share of hostile looks.

* * *

Talk about dumb.

In the split second it took for the gallon can of paint to slip from her fingers and smash into her toes, Catherine Walker knew her decision to pad around the house barefoot as she organized her remodeling supplies had been a huge mistake.

And the sharp pain that shot through her foot and set off bright pinpricks of light behind her eyes confirmed it.

Choking back a cry, she stared down at her crushed toes as the can rolled away. And came to the obvious conclusion.

Her do-it-yourself remodeling plans for the B and B she was scheduled to open in eight short weeks were hosed.

"What was that noise, Mom?"

Exiting the main house, Zach skidded to a stop in front of her in the breezeway that connected the two parts of their new home near Surfside. Soon to be known as Sheltering Shores Inn.

Maybe.

She cast another dubious eye at her foot, blinking back tears.

Without waiting for a reply, Zach squatted in front of her and examined her swelling toes.

"Wow! They're turning purple, Mom. Do they hurt?"

"Yeah." A lot.

"Should we call 911?"

He gave her a hopeful look. She knew he was desperate for some excitement, some activity to break the monotony of his days on this quiet byway they'd called home for the past three weeks. Their occasional trips to the grocery and hardware stores didn't provide enough variety for her inquisitive six-year-old. And he'd hated sitting through weddings, like the one she'd played at two weeks ago. But since their move from Atlanta, she'd been too busy settling in to do much exploring with him.

That was about to change, she conceded as she tried to put her weight on her foot and cringed. She didn't intend to summon an ambulance, but a trip to the ER seemed unavoidable.

"No, honey. I don't need 911. But I think I better have a doctor take a look at my foot."

"In town?"

"Yes."

"Can we stop at Downyflake before we come home?"

Already the local hangout, known for its sugar doughnuts—which had edged out Hershey's Kisses as her son's favorite treat—was high on his list of must-visit places whenever they ventured out.

"We'll see what time it is when we're through."

"Okay. Want me to get your purse?"

"That would be good. And grab my sandals, too, okay?"

While he headed back into the kitchen to retrieve the items, Catherine tested her foot again. If she put her weight on her heel, she could hobble as far as the car, she decided. But beyond that…

A sudden surge of panic swept over her, and she did her best to stifle it. She'd find a way to cope. She always did. Things would be okay.

They had to be.

"Here they are, Mom." Zach burst through the door, purse and shoes in hand. "You want to lean on me?"

Despite the pain that was intensifying with every passing minute, she dredged up a smile as she gazed down into his earnest, trusting face. What would she do without this little guy? If it hadn't been for him—and her music—she'd never have made it through the past two years. Yet she'd come so close to losing him, too. Fear clutched at her, twisting her stomach and renewing her resolve to make his safety her top priority.

"That would be nice, Zach. Thank you."

After she slipped her feet into her sandals, he moved beside her. She'd intended only to lay her hand on his shoulder, but she found herself leaning on him more than she expected as she locked the door and they headed for her Honda Civic, parked in front.

"I guess it hurts, huh, Mom?"

"A little. But the doctor will fix it up and I'll be good as new. Can you get your seat belt on by yourself?"

"Sure."

He hopped into the backseat while she took her place behind the wheel and carefully lifted her injured foot inside. As she put the key in the ignition, she checked on Zach. He was already strapped into the car they'd driven up from Atlanta, eager for an outing—no matter the destination.

She grimaced as she eased the car back, every little bump on the gravel drive reverberating through her foot. Zach was watching her face in the rearview mirror, his expression somber.

"I guess maybe you should have worn shoes when you were carrying those paint cans," he offered.

No kidding.

A tall, white-coated man with light brown hair entered the examining room at Cottage Hospital and smiled first at Zach. "Hey, big guy. How are you doing?"

The youngster shrugged. "Okay, I guess."

"Getting tired of sitting around?"

"Yeah."

"I hear you. Let's get your mom taken care of so you can go home."

He turned to Catherine and held out his hand. Mid-thirties, she estimated as he approached the examining table, with an appealing compassion in his blue eyes. He looked familiar, but she couldn't place him.

"Christopher Morgan, Mrs. Walker. Sorry it took me a while to get to you. We were dealing with some victims of a car accident who needed immediate attention."

She took his hand. "No problem. So what's the bad news?"

"Two broken toes."

Her shoulders drooped. The verdict wasn't a surprise, but she'd been hoping they might only be bruised. She'd even toyed with the idea of praying for that outcome, though she'd quickly dismissed that notion. Why bother? God hadn't come through for her the last time she'd sought His help.

"What does that mean in practical terms, Doctor?" She tried not to panic again, but it was difficult to remain calm when she had no idea how she was going to whip the inn into shape in time for her first customers.

"No strenuous activity involving your feet for the next six weeks."

"I suppose climbing up and down ladders falls into that category?"

He folded his arms across his chest. "Definitely."

She stared down at her elevated foot, which was surrounded by ice packs.

"Are you gonna put on a cast?" Zach interjected. "You know, the kind people draw on?"

"Nope. That's the good news." The doctor smiled at him, then redirected his attention to Catherine. "A hard-soled, sturdy shoe should do the trick. You need to protect your toes from further injury while they heal."

"I have some hiking boots."

"Those will work."

Good thing she'd thrown them into a box at the last minute instead of giving them to charity, as she'd been tempted to do, Catherine reflected. Although looking at them had evoked a bittersweet pang and reminded her of happy times never to return, the thought of cutting that link to David had been more painful than dealing with resurrected memories. So she'd kept them.

"Now let's talk treatment."

The doctor's voice drew her back to the present, and she shoved her melancholy thoughts into a dark corner of her mind.

"Expect quite a bit of bruising and swelling. Prop your foot on a pillow when you're sleeping, and stay off it as much as possible for the next few days at least—no prolonged standing or walking. Keep your foot elevated above your head, if possible. That will help reduce the swelling. For the first couple of days, put ice on it for fifteen to twenty minutes every hour or two. You can use a plastic bag filled with ice, but be sure to put a towel between it and your skin. Take an over-the-counter pain reliever if you need it. Any questions?"

"No."

He tipped his head. "I have one. Why did you ask about ladders a few minutes ago?"

She combed her fingers through her hair and expelled a frustrated breath. "I'm renovating a house I just bought that I plan to turn into a B and B. We've only been here three weeks, so I haven't gotten very far. And my first guests are arriving August 1."

"Are you doing the work yourself?" His eyebrows rose in surprise.

"Yes. Or I'd planned to, anyway. It's mostly cosmetic. Nothing too heavy, but it does require a lot of climbing up and down ladders." She sighed. "I guess I'll have to find someone to help if I want to be ready for opening day."

"I can help you, Mom," Zach volunteered.

She smiled and reached out to take his small hand. "I know, Zach. And you're a good worker.

But I'll need someone a little bigger, too, to carry heavy things and climb the ladder."

"If you're in the market for an extra pair of hands, I'd be happy to give you the name of my brother-in-law," the doctor offered. "He's new on the island, too. I know he has some training in carpentry and painting, and he's already done some work at our church."

Catherine sent him a grateful look. "That would be great. Thanks."

The doctor pulled a prescription pad out of his pocket and jotted a couple of lines. Stifling a yawn, he gave her a sheepish grin and handed it over. "Sorry about that. I just got back from my honeymoon yesterday, and I'm fighting a little jet lag."

Honeymoon.

The word conjured up a poignant image of white beaches, palm trees and a tall, sandy-haired man with love and laughter in his eyes.

It also reminded Catherine where she'd seen the doctor before. She'd played at his wedding two weeks ago. He'd looked quite different that day, in a tux instead of a white coat. Besides, her attention had been on her son, not the bride and groom, whose happiness had brought back bittersweet memories.

Somehow Catherine dredged up a smile. "Congratulations."

"Thanks. Let me help you off the table."

He freed her foot from the ice bags, waited while she gingerly swung her legs over the edge and supported her as she fitted her feet into her sandals.

"Is someone waiting to drive you home?"

"We drove ourselves," Zach piped up.

The doctor frowned. "Driving in your condition isn't the best idea."

It was all Catherine could do to hold her tears at bay now that her foot was flat on the floor again—and throbbing with pain. How could two little toes possibly hurt this much?

Summoning up a shaky smile, she brushed his concern aside. "I don't have far to go. Besides, my car's an automatic, and my right foot is fine."

"I'd feel better if you were a passenger instead of a driver. Isn't there anyone you could call?"

She didn't miss the subtle glance he cast toward her wedding ring.

"No."

At the finality in her tone, he capitulated. "Okay. I'll have one of the aides take you to your car in a wheelchair. But no more driving for a few days. Deal?"

"Deal."

Five minutes later, as Catherine maneuvered herself into her car with the help of the aide, she thought back to the doctor's question about whether there was someone who could assist her.

She wished she'd been able to answer in the affirmative. That she could pick up a phone and call the man who'd been the center of her world for eight glorious years.

But she was alone now, except for Zach.

And she always would be.

Because a broken heart was a whole lot harder to heal than two broken toes.

Chapter Two

Nathan braked to a stop on the side of the bike path as he approached Surfside and pulled out the directions he'd jotted down when Catherine Walker had called last night. Her street should be the next one on the left, he concluded, pocketing the slip of paper.

The three-mile bike ride from Nantucket town hadn't taken him nearly as long as he'd expected, so he slowed his speed as he turned off the main road and headed down the dirt lane. The houses here were spread much farther apart than the ones in town, and all were constructed of weathered clapboard. Although they were too far from the beach to offer a glimpse of the sea, they had a wide-open vista of the blue sky and felt a world removed from the tourist crowds and noise. He liked that.

He had no trouble spotting the house his potential boss had described. It was a bit unusual in that it consisted of two clapboard structures joined by a breezeway. The one on the left was a story and a half, Cape Cod in style, while the smaller section on the right appeared to be one level.

Unlike the houses closer to town or in 'Sconset, it didn't boast lush, well-tended gardens and tall privet hedges. Instead, it seemed to blend into the open, windswept terrain, as if it was a natural part of the landscape. He liked that, too.

Leaning his bike against the rail fence that separated the property from the dirt road, he walked up the gravel path to a front porch rimmed with budding hydrangea bushes. After ascending three steps, he rubbed his palms on his jeans and knocked on the door.

"Hey, Mom, he's here!"

The sound of a child's voice drifted through one of the front windows, which was open two or three inches. That was followed by the sound of eager, running footsteps. And a woman's voice.

"Wait for me, Zach. I'll open the door."

Zach.

Nathan had only the space of a few heartbeats, while he listened as a lock was slid back and a dead bolt turned, to process that name and come to a startling conclusion.

But it was more warning than the woman who opened the door was granted.

Stunned, Nathan stared at the wary violinist. The mother of the friendless, blond-haired little boy.

She stared back.

Several beats of silence passed.

Her son recovered first. A wide, welcoming smile split his face as he beamed up at the visitor. "Hey, Nathan! It's me, Zach, remember? From the wedding. You gave me your cake!"

Grateful for the distraction, Nathan tore his gaze away from the woman's startled green eyes and smiled down at the youngster. "Hi, champ. I'm surprised to see you again."

"Yeah. Me, too. Isn't this cool, Mom?"

One look told Nathan that *cool* didn't come anywhere close to describing Catherine Walker's reaction. Cautious, guarded, uncertain—those adjectives were more accurate. Placing a protective hand on her son's shoulder, she edged closer to him.

"Mr. Clay, I assume?"

"Yes."

She hesitated for another moment, as if still processing this peculiar coincidence and debating how to proceed. But at last she took a deep breath and stepped outside, pulling the door closed behind her. "All the work's in that building." She gestured toward the smaller structure on the other side of the breezeway. "I'll show you around and you can put together an estimate."

He followed her in silence, noting her limp—and the sturdy, somewhat clunky hiking boots that were out of place with her slim capri pants. When they reached the porch steps, she descended slowly, one at a time, bottom lip caught between her teeth, features contorted with pain.

In his thirty-four years, he'd had more than his share of cuts, scrapes and broken bones. And he knew how much they could hurt. For an instant he was tempted to take her arm in a steadying grip. But he quashed the impulse at once, shoving his hands into the pockets of his jeans instead as he followed at a nonthreatening distance. If he so much as breathed on her, he suspected she'd send him packing.

"My brother-in-law told me about your accident," he offered. "I'm sorry."

"I'll live. But it's not very convenient."

"She dropped a can of paint on her foot in there." Zach pointed to the breezeway, throwing the words over his shoulder as he trotted along beside his mother, his hand firmly held in hers. "I heard it all the way in the living room. Then her toes got purple. And they puffed up. They look really gross. And she can't walk very…"

"Zach." Catherine's quiet but firm tone cut him off. "I'm sure Mr. Clay doesn't want to hear about my toes."

"He might. Did you ever break anything?" Zach directed the question over his shoulder.

"A couple of fingers once."

"Yeah?" Zach gave him an interested glance. "How?"

He should have seen that question coming, Nathan realized in dismay. No way did he intend to share that bit of background with this duo. Telling this wary woman they'd been smashed by a police officer's baton wasn't likely to win him any brownie points.

Pulling open the door of the breezeway, Catherine saved him by changing the subject.

"Let me explain the project." She stepped inside and he followed. "I plan to use the smaller part of the house as a B and B. It's already set up as guest quarters, with two large bedrooms, each with a private bath and a separate entrance. However, it's in desperate need of some TLC. I have guests booked beginning August 1, which would have given me plenty of time to get the work done myself. But now I'm going to need some help."

She took a key out of her pocket, fitted it into one of the two doors in the breezeway that led into the structure and pushed it open.

Nathan followed her in. The empty room was large and boasted a vaulted ceiling, but evidence of disrepair was obvious. Some of the drywall was damaged, paint was flaking off in several areas and the stained carpet smelled musty.

"The other room's worse," she told him as she limped over to the bathroom and pushed the door open. "It has peeling psychedelic wallpaper that will have to be stripped—meaning lots of drywall repair, I suspect. I also want to install Pergo wood-grained flooring in both rooms. Any experience with that?

"No. But I'm a fast learner."

She gave a slight nod. "I installed some a few years ago in our old house. It's not that hard. I can guide you through it. Maybe even help by that point." She flipped on the light in the bathroom. "These aren't as bad. They need more redecorating than repair.

He moved close enough to get a glimpse of a basic bathroom over her shoulder. The fixtures and tile floor appeared to be in decent shape, but the space was bland.

Stepping back into the room again, he planted his fists on his hips and gave it a dubious scan.

"Believe it or not, Mr. Clay, this room has great potential."

At Catherine's wry comment, Nathan felt heat

rise on his neck. He hadn't meant for his skepticism to be so obvious.

"I'll have to take your word for that. The repairs I can do. The decorating…" He shook his head. "Making this room appealing would be beyond my talents."

"I can take care of that part. I used to be an interior designer." She moved toward the door. "Let me show you the other room."

When he leaned around her to open the door, she jerked back.

"Sorry. I didn't mean to startle you." He eased away, pulling the door wide, wondering again why she was so skittish.

A soft flush colored her cheeks, as if she was embarrassed by her reaction. "Thanks."

She limped through, tugging Zach along with her, but he pulled free. "We're not crossing a street, Mom. And there aren't any strangers around. We know Nathan now. You don't have to hold my hand."

As he dashed ahead to wait at the adjacent door, Catherine's flush deepened. Averting her head, she led the way to the second door in silence, inserted the key in the lock and pushed it open. Gesturing Nathan inside, she remained on the threshold as he and her son entered the room.

Catherine's assessment had been correct, Nathan

concluded, inspecting the sorry wallpaper and faded vinyl floor covering. This room was in worse shape.

He shook his head. "I hope the part of the house you're living in is in better condition than this."

"Nope," Zach chimed in. "There were spiders in my room when we moved in. Yuck!"

"Just a few. And they're gone now," Catherine corrected her son before answering Nathan's question. "It's livable until we get the guest quarters fixed up."

Her response suggested it wasn't much better than the room in which he was standing. Making him wonder what had compelled her to buy such a fixer-upper.

As if she'd read his mind, she folded her arms across her chest and regarded him from the threshold. "Prices are very high on the island. Especially property. This was the best I could afford. Besides, it met my criteria of keeping our home and the guest quarters separate. I wanted to maintain some privacy."

She glanced around the guest room, her features tightening in pain as she shifted her weight to relieve the pressure on her injured foot. "This property used to be owned by an older couple, but they hadn't visited for a long time. And this section has been ignored for years. According to the Realtor, after the woman's husband died she became too feeble to travel. But she hung on to this place because it held a lot of happy memories for her."

"Kind of like you kept those hiking boots you're wearing, huh, Mom?"

At Zach's comment, she sucked in a sharp breath. Before she could recover, the youngster continued.

"My mom and dad used to go hiking a lot when I was little. Mom says my dad used to carry me on his back. That was when we lived in Atlanta, before my dad went to heaven."

As Zach's last comment echoed in the empty room, Nathan tried not to let his shock register on his face.

Catherine's husband was dead.

Now he knew why Zach had been with her at the wedding instead of at home with his dad. And why she'd planned to tackle this job alone.

It also explained the deep sadness in her eyes when their gazes met for a brief, compelling instant before she jerked hers away and took a clumsy step back.

"So…do you want to bid on the job?"

"Yes." His response was immediate. The work was within his abilities, and he wanted to spend more time with these two people who seemed in such desperate need of a friend.

"Could you get back to me by tomorrow with a number? I need to move on this quickly."

"I can give you an estimate now. For labor,

anyway. We can adjust it if the project is finished sooner." He'd been doing some mental calculations as they'd looked over the structure, and he'd already estimated the number of hours it would take to complete the work.

Her eyebrows rose. "That's fast."

He shrugged. "I know about how much time I'll need. The math after that is easy. And if I finish sooner, the cost will be less." He named a dollar amount.

When she frowned, he shoved his hands into his pockets. "Look, if that's too much, we can negotiate. And if you need a reference, the pastor at the church I attend can vouch for me. I've done a couple of jobs for him in the past three weeks."

"It's not the reference. It's the bid. I probably shouldn't say this, but—that's on the low side for Nantucket. Prices here are high for everything."

"It seems like a fair wage to me. And I don't have a lot of expenses."

"Well…if you're sure. Can you start Monday?"

"Yes." A surge of elation washed over him. He'd gotten a job! Maybe not much of one. But it was a start. And that's all he needed right now. Just someone to give him a chance. To believe in him. To trust him.

Zach grinned up at him. "Maybe you can be my friend, Nathan."

"Honey, his name is Mr. Clay," Catherine corrected.

"Actually, Nathan is fine with me if it's okay with you." He managed to coax his tense lips into a smile. "I'm not much into formalities."

He waited for her to reciprocate. Hoped she would. But she didn't.

"If that's what you prefer." She moved away from the door, and Zach and Nathan exited. Once they were out, she locked it and tucked the key into the pocket of her capris. "I'm going to put my foot up again. We'll see you Monday. Come on, Zach."

She started to reach for his hand, but when he backed off, she let her arm drop to her side. Then she headed for the door that led into the main house, on the other side of the breezeway.

Zach's farewell was much warmer and delivered with a megawatt smile. "Next time you come, I'll show you the toy soldiers my grandma and grandpa sent me from Germany, okay?"

"That sounds great."

Beaming, the youngster trotted off to follow his mother inside. A moment later, Nathan heard the distinctive sound of a lock sliding into place.

Retracing his steps down the gravel path in front of the house, he mounted his bike and set off for town, mulling over all he'd learned today—and wrestling with a new question.

Why had Catherine Walker moved far away from her home to start a new life in a rundown house on an island where everyone was a stranger?

As Nathan pedaled toward town, the answer eluded him. Yet one thing did become clear. While some of his questions about the beautiful violinist and her charming son had been answered today, a lot more had cropped up to take their place.

On the plus side, though, if all went well with the job he'd have ample opportunity to find some answers.

No. Scratch that. There was no *if* about it. Everything *would* go well. He was done messing up his life. He might not be able to delete the dark chapters, but he was determined to fill the ones yet to be written with light and grace.

And maybe, with God's help, he could help a wary woman and a lonely little boy do the same.

Chapter Three

❧

"My goodness! That's amazing."

At Edith's comment, Nathan swiveled in his seat, paintbrush in hand. His landlady was staring at the canvas on the easel he'd set up in her garden, just outside his rental cottage. Her lips were slightly parted in astonishment, the chocolate-chip cookies and glass of milk she was holding apparently forgotten.

Feeling self-conscious, Nathan picked up a rag and wiped a smear of paint off his hand.

"I appreciate your enthusiasm, but I don't have any training."

"Who cares? You have talent. That's even better." She moved closer to examine the painting of a little boy on a beach, his head tipped back to the sun, arms lifted, his face the embodiment of joy and innocence and optimism.

"I saw the pen-and-ink drawing you did of The Devon Rose as a wedding present for J.C. and Heather, but I had no idea you were such a talented painter."

Although the praise pleased him, Nathan felt uncomfortable. He'd had so little affirmation in his life, he had no idea how to respond. "I'm not that good."

"Baloney. I'm no artist, but I know a…"

The half-moon gate to Edith's backyard opened, and her neighbor, Kate MacDonald Cole, walked through.

"Kate…come over here!" Edith called.

Much to Nathan's dismay, the red-haired charter-boat captain joined the group. He wasn't used to an audience.

"Look at this." Edith gestured to his painting. "Is that amazing or what?"

The younger woman moved closer to peruse the work in progress. When at last she transferred her attention to him, Nathan could tell by her expression that she was impressed.

"I agree with Edith. Did you paint this here in the yard?"

"No. I did most of it at Dionis Beach over the past couple of weeks. But it only needs a few more touches, so I decided to finish it up here."

"How long have you been painting?"

"Not long. I didn't have access to any good painting supplies in...until I came here. I did pencil sketches and pen-and-ink drawings."

Kate gave him a steady look. "You're good enough to do this professionally."

Heat suffused Nathan's neck. "I don't think so."

"You listen to Kate, young man," Edith chimed in. "Her late husband was a very successful artist. She knows talent when she sees it."

"I'll tell you what..." Kate propped her hands on her hips and surveyed the painting. "Why don't I mention you to the owner of the gallery where Mac sold his work? She's always on the prowl for up-and-coming artists. That way, if you decide you want to market your work, she'll already know your name."

"I don't know...I'd planned to focus on carpentry and house-painting jobs for a while." Those were the skills he'd learned in the prison program. The ones he was comfortable with. Painting had always been just a hobby, a way to pass the time. And to express the emotions locked in his heart.

"Why in the world would you want to paint a house when you can do this?" Edith gestured toward the canvas.

"To put food on the table?" Nathan flashed her a quick grin.

Kate chuckled. "Good point. It's not easy to

make a living as an artist. But you'll never know if you don't try, as Mac used to say. How about I mention your name, and you take it from there? Or not. It's the Blue Water Gallery on India Street. The owner is Monica Stevens."

"Okay. Thanks. I'll think about it."

"Are the girls ready, Edith?" Kate asked.

"Yes. They're in the kitchen, taking the chocolate-chip cookies off the pans."

Kate rolled her eyes. "Why do I think they're going to pick at their dinner tonight?"

"I told them to eat only two each."

"And you've been out here how long?"

"Five minutes."

"I rest my case. See you later, Nathan."

With a wave, she jogged toward Edith's back door.

"I better go in and referee." Edith set the milk and a plate of cookies on the table beside Nathan. "These are for you."

Ever since he'd arrived, his Lighthouse Lane landlady had been dropping treats off at the cottage his siblings had rented for him in the corner of her yard, starting with the pumpkin bread that had been waiting for him when he'd arrived. He was beginning to feel guilty.

"I appreciate the cookies, but you don't have to keep feeding me, you know."

She waved his comment aside. "Someone needs to. You could stand to put on a few pounds. Get Heather to give you some of her scones with clotted cream and strawberry preserves. That'll do the trick. And I have the hips to prove it." She patted the ample anatomy in question and chuckled. "But they're worth every pound. See you later, young man."

With a flutter of fingers, she retreated to her house.

As silence descended in the quiet, private yard shielded from the world by a tall privet hedge, Nathan picked up a warm-from-the-oven cookie and took a bite. Nirvana, he thought, savoring the burst of flavor from the gooey chocolate. It was funny how simple treats—or acts of kindness, like the painting supplies from his siblings that he'd found waiting for him in the cottage when he'd arrived—could bring a sudden lump to his throat. As could the heady scent of freedom, the trill of a bird and an endless expanse of sea or sky.

In hindsight, he wondered how he'd survived all those years of confinement—and the demeaning, soul-shattering experience of being treated like an object rather than a person.

Yet the latter hadn't been confined to his decade behind bars, he acknowledged as the cookie caught in his throat. That legacy went back far longer.

Taking a swig of milk to dislodge the lump of dough stuck in his windpipe, he forced his thoughts in more pleasant directions.

Unbidden, an image of Catherine Walker and her son flashed through his mind. He still couldn't get over the fact that their paths had crossed again. And based on her expression when she'd opened her door yesterday, she'd felt the same way. Except she hadn't seemed especially pleased about the odd twist of fate.

Yet she'd offered him the job.

Meaning he could look forward to a lot more interaction with the wary violinist and her charming son. And if he was very lucky, maybe one day down the road her wariness would subside and he'd find the answers to some of his questions about the intriguing—and appealing—duo.

"Zach! It's lunchtime!"

As she called her son, Catherine carefully lifted her injured foot off the wicker ottoman in the breezeway, where she'd had it propped all morning. She hadn't planned to hover over Nathan during his first morning on the job, but Zach had balked at her plan to keep him inside for a few days while she observed the newcomer from a distance. In the end she'd capitulated, setting herself up in the breezeway with a stack of decorating books and a pad of paper so she could play with layouts for the two B and B rooms—and keep an eye on her new carpenter.

She'd soon realized, however, that her concern had been unnecessary. If anything, Zach had disrupted Nathan's life rather than vice versa. Not that you'd know it by watching the man, though. He had the patience of Job. And he was good with kids.

Rising from the lounge chair, Catherine took a moment to steady herself before trekking to the kitchen to fix lunch. The two male voices continued to converse in the psychedelic room, one calm and mellow, the other high-pitched and animated. The exchange had been going almost nonstop all morning.

At one point, assuming Zach was getting in Nathan's way, Catherine had stepped to the door and cautioned him not to bother the older man. But Nathan had won a friend for life when he'd responded that Zach was helping him—and doing a good job. At the compliment, her son's chest had puffed out and he'd displayed the bucket of wallpaper scraps he'd peeled off the bottom of the wall.

It was the kind of considerate thing David would have done, Catherine reflected as she limped toward the kitchen door, a pain pill high on her priority list. Yet no pain pill could relieve the ache in her heart as she thought about the man she'd loved—and the father Zach would never know.

Pausing at the door to call her son again, she fought down a wave of despondency. Two years ago, everyone had told her the grief would dissipate over time. But why had no one warned her that the loneliness and sense of loss would intensify?

"Zach!"

Her second summons came out shaky—but it produced results. The little boy appeared moments later, followed by Nathan.

"Sorry he didn't come on the first call. I was cleaning up his hands. They were a little sticky from the wallpaper paste." Nathan gave her a probing look. "Everything okay?"

"Yes. Fine." She pasted on a smile, trying to squelch the uncomfortable feeling that this stranger had just tapped into her deepest well of sadness. "But I don't want to be late putting Zach down for his nap."

"Oh, Mom." Zach thrust out his chin and folded his arms across his chest. "I'm too old for naps."

A pulsating pain—a twin to the one in her foot—began to pound in her head, and Catherine rubbed her temple as a wave of nausea swept over her. "We're not going to argue about this, Zach. Go into the kitchen. Now!" The words came out sharper than she intended, and when tears welled in Zach's eyes, her nausea ratcheted up a notch.

"You don't have to get mad about it."

"I'm not mad. I'm…" All at once, Catherine's stomach revolted. Covering her mouth with her hand, she turned and clumped toward the bathroom as fast as her broken toes would allow.

She made it just in time to lose whatever breakfast remained in her stomach.

When she finally stopped retching, a soft knock sounded on the bathroom door.

"Mrs. Walker? Are you all right?"

She closed her eyes. Nathan had followed her in. Meaning he'd not only witnessed her bad temper with Zach, he's also heard her empty the contents of her stomach into the toilet.

Not an auspicious beginning for their employer/ employee relationship.

"Mrs. Walker?" The concern in his voice edged up a notch.

"I'm okay." She took a deep breath. One part of her wasn't happy he'd trespassed into their private quarters. Another part was touched that he'd cared enough to take that chance. She wasn't sure which reaction was stronger. And she wasn't in any shape to figure it out. "Where's Zach?"

"He's waiting in the kitchen. It took a couple of Hershey's Kisses from the bowl on the counter to convince him to stay put, though."

So much for his lunch, Catherine thought with

a sigh. But at least the bribe had bought her a few minutes to get herself together.

Gripping the vanity for support, she examined her reflection. Not good. All the color had vanished from her face, and small beads of sweat rimmed her upper lip. She could try and buy herself a few more minutes, but she doubted her appearance was going to improve anytime soon. Resigned, she snagged a tissue, wiped off the moisture, straightened her shoulders and swung the door open.

Nathan sized her up in one swift but thorough scan. "You don't look too good. Any idea what's going on?"

"Too many pain pills is my guess." She propped a weary shoulder against the doorframe. "I don't take any medicine as a rule, and I've been doubling up on the dosage. I felt a little queasy last night, too."

"That could be it. Why don't you lie down for a while?"

She tried to smile. Failed. "Not an option. I have a six-year-old to feed."

Several beats of silence passed as he regarded her. "I could do that for you. If it's something simple." The smile he gave her seemed a bit stiff. Like a little-used window that had to be coaxed open. "I'm afraid I never learned many cooking skills."

Under normal circumstances, Catherine would have refused his offer. She didn't relegate Zach's care to anyone. Nor did she allow strangers in her home. But with a throbbing head, a throbbing foot and legs so shaky she wasn't certain they'd keep her upright much longer, these weren't normal circumstances. Not by a long shot.

Rather than labor over the decision, she told herself she ought to be grateful that providence or fate or simple luck had provided a set of helping hands today.

"Can you handle a peanut butter and jelly sandwich?"

His smile hitched up a notch. "If you direct the process, I'm sure I can manage."

He seemed to understand that much as she might want to take his advice and lie down, there was no way she intended to leave him in her home—nor with her son—unsupervised. She was glad he'd discerned that—and hadn't taken offense. It made things easier. Less awkward. And there was no hurt in his eyes this time, as there had been when she'd rebuffed his gesture of friendship toward her son at the wedding.

Relieved, she tucked her hair behind her ear. "That works."

He stepped aside to let her pass as she started down the hall, but she hadn't gone more than three steps when her good leg buckled. He was behind her in an instant, his hands firm on her upper arms, supporting her.

Fingers splayed against the wall, she drew an unsteady breath. "Sorry. I guess that little episode took more out of me than I thought."

Without releasing his grip, he stepped beside her. "You've had a rough few days. Why don't you lean on me and we'll get you situated in the kitchen?"

The notion of leaning on anyone didn't sit well with her, but she didn't have much choice. Not if she wanted to make it to the kitchen on her feet instead of her knees. "Okay."

He slipped his right arm around her shoulders, and she moved closer to him, clinging to his left hand.

As they slowly traversed the short passageway, Catherine discovered a couple of things. Despite his thinness, Nathan was strong. She could feel power in the sinewy muscles that bunched in his forearm, in the solid chest that brushed her shoulder, in the lean fingers that gripped her forearm. And he was also tall, towering at least six or seven inches above her five-foot-five frame.

Usually big, strong men scared her.

For some reason, this one didn't.

When they entered the kitchen, Zach looked up

from a small pile of incriminating silver paper, his guilty expression morphing to concern. "How come you're so white?"

"Your mom's toes are hurting a lot, and her stomach isn't too happy about the medicine she's taking to help them feel better." Nathan stepped in before she could respond, and Catherine let him. She also let him guide her to one of the kitchen chairs. And she didn't protest when he retrieved the cushion from the breezeway and lifted her foot to an adjacent chair, his fingers warm and gentle as he settled the soft pad under it.

A little quiver that had nothing to do with nausea rippled through her stomach, and Catherine frowned. What in the world was that all about?

"How does a peanut butter and jelly sandwich sound?" Nathan directed his question to Zach.

Her son sidled a guilty look in her direction. "I'm not real hungry."

Nathan swiped up the incriminating silver papers and deposited them in the trash can. "You must be. Hard workers have big appetites. And you're a hard worker, aren't you?"

"Yeah." Zach wandered over to the table and sat, chin in palm, watching Nathan.

"I thought so." He turned toward Catherine. "Peanut butter?"

"In the cabinet on your right. Jelly's in the

fridge. Bread's on the counter, by the toaster." She motioned tiredly to her left, the spare response all she could manage.

She watched as he went about his task with an admirable efficiency of motion. It was the same approach he took with his work. She'd noticed it when she'd stopped in a few times this morning to make sure Zach wasn't getting in his way.

But as she took a closer look at him for the first time, she noticed some other things, as well. Flecks of silver in his neatly trimmed brown hair. Fine lines at the corners of his eyes. Small scars on his temple and chin. Brown eyes that looked as if they'd seen way too much bad stuff, confirming the impression she'd had at the wedding.

Guessing his age to be midthirties, Catherine couldn't help wondering what struggles this quiet man had endured to earn those premature signs of age. Were they as traumatic, as life-changing, as her own? Were they the reason he was trying to make a new start on this island, as she was?

"How about some milk to go with that?" Nathan set the finished sandwich in front of Zach and raised an eyebrow at Catherine.

Refocusing on the present, she nodded.

Without waiting for Zach to respond, Nathan pulled a gallon jug out of the refrigerator, poured a glass and placed it beside the youngster's plate.

"What're you eating?" Zach inspected his sandwich as he queried Nathan.

"I brought a turkey sandwich from home."

"Why don't you go get it? That way, we can eat together."

Nathan cast a quick glance at Catherine and rested his hands on the back of one of the two empty chairs. "I think I'll have lunch later. After you're finished."

Plunking an elbow on the table, Zach propped his chin in his hand again and pressed a finger into his sandwich, creating dimples in the soft white bread. "It's no fun to eat by yourself."

There was a cue here for her, Catherine realized. She could take it—invite this stranger to dine with her son—or remain silent and let him walk out. To eat alone.

Two weeks ago, if someone had told her she'd even consider inviting a man she'd known for only three days to eat in her kitchen, she would have dismissed the comment as absurd. She didn't trust easily. Not anymore. But Nathan had come to her via a respected E.R. doctor. And he'd done some work at a church, offered to give her the name of his pastor. As far as she was concerned, those were good character references.

In her heart, however, she knew that wasn't the only reason her attitude toward this man was softening. Even though she knew nothing about

Nathan's background, she couldn't shake the feeling that somehow, in some way, they might be kindred spirits. And her instincts also told her that this man, who had charmed her son with his patience and kindness, possessed a gentle, caring spirit incapable of inflicting pain.

When the silence lengthened, Nathan started to turn away. But not before she caught a flash of sorrow in his eyes that tugged at her soul. Again. And pricked her conscience. Again.

This was her chance to try and make amends for the hurt her unfriendliness had inflicted at the wedding reception, she realized.

"Wait!"

He cast a glance over his shoulder.

"If you're hungry now, why don't you eat with Zach? Unless you'd rather spend some time alone on your lunch break."

He gave a slight shake of his head, and gratitude softened those velvet-brown irises. "I've had plenty of time alone. I'd welcome some company over lunch."

His response intrigued her, but when he offered nothing else, she gestured to the refrigerator. "Help yourself to some soda. And there are a few homemade brownies left on that foil-covered plate on the counter. You and Zach can divide them up. Then it's naptime for you, young man."

Zach scrunched up his face. "I hate naps. I'd rather help Nathan."

Leaning over, Nathan rested his forearms along the top of the chair back, putting him closer to eye-level with Zach. "I'm going to work on the ceiling this afternoon anyway, champ. You can help me again with the wallpaper tomorrow morning. How does that sound?"

Was this a sudden change of plan? Catherine wondered. Designed to make the nap more palatable by reassuring her son he wouldn't be missing anything? If so, she hoped Nathan's psychology worked. She wasn't up to any more battles today.

"Okay, I guess." Zach sounded more resigned than enthusiastic.

To sweeten the pot, Catherine touched his hand. "I'm going to lie down this afternoon, too, for an hour or two. How about if we nap together?"

His eyes brightened. "In your bed?"

She'd hoped that would do the trick. Sleeping with Mom was a rare treat, and she didn't bestow it often. The child psychologist had discouraged her from making it a habit, stressing the importance of returning to a normal routine as soon as possible. Besides, there were too many nights when she still woke up crying. Or shaking. Zach didn't need to witness that.

"Yes. In my bed."

"Cool!" Zach went back to eating with renewed enthusiasm. "You want to take a nap with us, too, Nathan? It might be a little crowded, but I bet we could all fit."

Heat surged on Catherine's neck, and she made a pretense of adjusting the laces on her elevated hiking boot.

"I have work to do, champ."

Nathan's husky reply did nothing to quell the unexpected flurry of butterflies Zach's comment had set off in her stomach. Fortunately he exited to retrieve his lunch, giving her a chance to compose herself. And when he returned, he kept the conversation focused on the remodeling project.

Once lunch was finished and he and Zach had polished off all the remaining brownies, Nathan went back to work with a nod in her direction and a quiet thank-you for the dessert and soda.

Fifteen minutes later, with Zach cuddled up beside her and already drifting off, her own eyelids began to grow heavy. Until a sudden realization drew her back from the brink of sleep.

For the first time in two years, she hadn't double-checked the locks on every door before lying down.

Snuggling closer to Zach, she told herself she ought to get up and secure the house.

But she didn't.

Because oddly enough, despite the presence of a stranger on her property, she felt safe.

Chapter Four

On Friday, as Nathan tapped the lid closed on the can containing the soft-ochre–colored paint Catherine had chosen for the psychedelic room, Zach planted his chubby hands on his hips and inspected the transformed space.

"This looks real good, Nathan."

Standing, he did his own survey. And came to the same conclusion. Although the flooring still needed to be laid, the rest of the room was ready for decorating.

"Thanks, champ. I couldn't have done it without you."

A glow suffused the little boy's face. "I like helping. Mom says I'm a good helper."

"She's right. I'm going to run over to the house and tell her I'm leaving, okay?"

"Okay. You want me to put your tools back in your toolbox while you're gone?"

Nathan scanned the room. One of his ground rules was that Zach wasn't to touch any tool without asking permission. And the little boy had followed it to the letter. But nothing lethal was lying around. Just a hammer, a paint-can opener and a couple of screwdrivers. "Sure. I'll be back in a minute."

As he exited the room, Nathan was pleased by the progress he'd made during his first week on the job—both with the room and with his employer. She'd begun to relax around him. To hover less. To trust him with Zach. That meant a lot. As did the routine they'd all fallen into of sharing their lunch at a glass-topped wicker table in the breezeway. Their conversation was always impersonal, focused mostly on the renovation, but the normalcy of it, and the sense of acceptance he felt, were a balm to his soul.

Crossing the breezeway, he could see Catherine through the screen door. She was angled away from him, arms akimbo, shoulders taut. As he approached, he heard her expel a frustrated breath before setting a jar on the counter.

He tapped on the door. "Looks like round one went to the jar."

She twisted toward him and gave a rueful shrug. "Try round three. I think I'm down for the count."

"Would you like me to give it a try?"

"Can't hurt."

"May I?" He gestured to the door. She hadn't asked him in since the day she'd gotten sick, and though her wary manner was softening, he didn't want to do anything to make her nervous.

"Sure."

She picked up the jar and met him halfway across the room, limping a little less than she had on Monday.

"How are the toes today?" He took the jar of spaghetti sauce as he asked the question.

"The swelling has gone down, and they don't hurt as much. Keeping them elevated helps a lot. But I don't like sitting around."

That didn't surprise him. Catherine struck him as a take-charge, get-it-done kind of woman.

He took a firm grip on the lid, preparing to give it a strong twist. "Well, maybe by next week you…"

His stopped midsentence as the lid came off far more easily than he expected and spaghetti sauce spewed all over the front of his gray T-shirt, dripping onto the floor at his feet.

Catherine gave a little shriek and took a quick step back.

Recovering from his surprise, Nathan set the jar on the counter and sent her an apologetic look.

"Sorry about that. I think I'm wearing your dinner. If you have a dish towel, I'll…"

Behind him, the screen door opened. "Hey, Mom, I heard you yell. What…"

As Nathan swiveled toward Zach, the little boy froze. In the space of a few heartbeats, every ounce of color drained from his face and he began to shake.

Alarmed, Nathan took a step toward him. "Hey, champ, it's okay."

The boy jerked back, his breath coming in shallow puffs.

"Oh, God!"

Nathan heard Catherine's murmured, anguished comment a second before she brushed past him, headed for her son. Wincing as she dropped to one knee in front of him, she pulled him close.

"I'm here, Zach. Hold on to me. It's okay. Nathan spilled some spaghetti sauce on his T-shirt. That's all. It's just spaghetti sauce. I guess we'll have to eat something else for dinner, huh? How does pizza sound? Would you like that?"

No response. The little boy continued to shake, his eyes glazed.

Nathan had no idea what was going on. Why was Zach so upset?

But that question could wait. At the moment, he was more interested in comforting a traumatized little boy and his frantic mother.

Stripping off the stained T-shirt that had apparently caused Zach's distress, he used it to wipe up the spaghetti sauce on the floor, then tossed it into the sink before joining the duo huddled near the screen door.

"What can I do to help, Mrs. Walker?"

She shook her head, still clinging to her son. "Nothing. I just need to calm him down before he hyperventilates." She backed off a bit to examine the boy's face. "Zach, honey, it's okay. Everybody's fine." She stroked his hair, his cheeks, his hands as she spoke. "Nathan's not hurt. He's right here."

Nathan dropped to their level, balancing on the balls of his feet. Following his instincts, he cocooned one of Zach's hands in his, his stomach contracting at the child's obvious terror. He could feel Catherine quivering beside him as well, fighting her own panic. "Hey, champ, did you finish putting away all the tools?" He kept his voice gentle, soothing—the way he wished an understanding adult would have talked him through his own childhood traumas.

No response.

He tried again.

"I was thinking that next week you could help me paint, if your mom says it's okay. Do you know how to paint?"

A flicker of awareness dawned in the child's blue eyes, the glaze dissipating slightly.

"It's okay with me if you want to help Nathan paint, Zach." Catherine jumped in, following his lead. "I might join you myself. Maybe we could have a painting party. Would you like that?"

Zach blinked. Sucked in a sharp breath. Then he gripped Nathan's hand and stared at him wide-eyed. "I saw blood."

His quavery words jolted Zach.

"No, honey. It was spaghetti sauce." Catherine ran her fingers through his fine blond hair. "Nathan spilled it all over his shirt. Like you spilled that jar of applesauce when we first moved here, remember? But it's all cleaned up now. And I think we'll have pizza for dinner instead. Would you like that?"

A shudder passed through Zach and he tightened his grip on Nathan's hand, exhibiting surprising strength for such a little thing. "Will you stay?"

Nathan deferred to Catherine with a silent look.

Unlike the day of the lunch invitation, she didn't hesitate. "If you can, it would help."

He didn't hesitate, either. "I'll stay."

"Thanks." Her grateful gaze met his for a brief second before she reached for Zach, who was still way too pale. "How about you lie down for a few minutes while I get the pizza ready?"

For once he didn't argue. But instead of folding himself into his mother's embrace, he lifted his arms to Nathan. "Will you carry me?"

Taken aback, Nathan checked with Catherine again.

"If you don't mind. It will help reassure him you're okay," she said softly.

He swallowed past the lump in his throat. "I don't mind in the least."

Wrapping his arms around Zach, he hoisted the boy onto his hip and stood, then extended a hand to Catherine. "I bet your toes didn't appreciate that position."

With a slight grimace, she accepted his hand and rose. "They'll be okay. Let me show you to Zach's room."

She led the way down the hall, limping more than she had since early in the week. And she took the stairs to the second floor very slowly.

Meaning she was hurting a lot more than she'd admitted.

The little boy shifted in his arms, emitting a soft sigh, and nestled closer to his heart. Nathan's throat constricted as he stroked a comforting hand over Zach's back. In his whole life, he'd never held a child. But the boy felt right in his arms. And good.

Catherine paused to catch her breath on the

landing of the dormered second floor, and he took the opportunity to get the lay of the land. It looked like the house had three bedrooms—a large master bedroom on his right, crammed with unopened boxes and furniture, and two smaller bedrooms on the left. The closest one contained a twin bed, and he started toward it.

"No…Zach's room is next door, at the back of the house," Catherine corrected him.

He gave the first room a quick inspection before continuing on. In addition to a twin bed, it contained a small dresser, chest, nightstand and straight chair. The bare walls were in desperate need of paint, the windows were curtainless, and the scuffed hardwood floor cried out for refinishing.

Zach's assessment a few days ago of the state of the main house had been right on.

Yuck.

The second floor was bad. And while he hadn't seen much of the first floor, the kitchen spoke volumes. The appliances were outdated, the flooring was cracked and the Formica countertop was chipped.

He couldn't imagine anyone who'd been an interior decorator living in this environment.

And interior decorator or not, Catherine deserved better.

"You can set him on the bed, Nathan."

Cradling Zach's head, he eased through the door to the adjacent room.

Once over the threshold, he stopped in surprise. Not only was this room bigger than Catherine's, it had been fully decorated—and with an imaginative hand. The walls were painted a cheery yellow, and a large throw rug featuring a parade of animals in primary colors hid much of the worn hardwood floor. Canvas swags at the windows were draped over stuffed giraffe heads, and the bedspread was done in a zebra pattern. Throw pillows shaped like safari hats were propped against the headboard, and a child-height coat rack was topped by silk palm leaves.

It was a little boy's dream room.

"Wow." He didn't know what else to say.

The whisper of a smile softened Catherine's tense features as she entered behind him and threw back the covers. "He's been into zoos and animals and safaris for the past year. When we moved, I decided to recreate his room here. I thought having one familiar place in the house might ease the transition."

She stepped aside, and Nathan moved forward to lay the boy down. But the youngster tightened his grip around Nathan's neck.

"Are you leaving?" His words came out slurred with sleep.

"No. I'll be downstairs. Remember, we're going to have pizza when you wake up."

"Oh, yeah. Mom?" He looked over Nathan's shoulder, and Nathan felt Catherine come up behind him.

"I'm here, honey."

"Okay. Just checking."

His eyelids drifted closed, and Nathan set him down, then stepped back as Catherine drew the covers up to Zach's chin. Leaning close, she pressed her lips to his forehead, brushing back a wisp of his blond hair with fingers that still trembled.

"I think I'll stay for a few minutes to make sure he doesn't wake up." She stood and faced Nathan across the bed, her gaze flicking to his bare chest. And lingering for a second on the jagged scar on the upper right side.

He'd forgotten about that. And the fact he was shirtless.

Time to exit.

"I'll wait downstairs."

She gave a slight nod and turned back toward her son.

As Nathan retraced his steps, determined to rinse out his shirt and put it back on before she reappeared, he cast another look at the room where she slept. There was a forlornness about it, a sadness, that seeped into his pores. The feeling of aloneness was so visceral it permeated his soul.

Yet despite the tragedy she'd endured—and only a tragedy could have induced the kind of scene he'd just witnessed with Zach—she was carrying on. Trying to make a new life for herself and her son.

He admired that. A lot.

But he was also curious.

And he hoped that in addition to offering him some pizza tonight, she might also offer him a glimpse into her heart.

As Nathan disappeared down the steps, Zach's even breathing told Catherine her son was already sound asleep. That it was safe to go downstairs.

But *safe* was a relative term.

Because a man with questions in his eyes would be waiting for her.

And that was scary.

She limped over to the window and stared up at the deep blue sky. Not once in the past two years had she talked about the traumatic event that had changed her life. An event that still felt as raw as if it had happened yesterday.

Maybe it always would.

As she watched, a gull soared high above her on a wind current, suspended halfway between earth and sky, belonging to neither. That's how she'd felt for the past twenty-four months. In limbo. Apart. Isolated.

She'd shared her feelings with no one, though. Not her high-powered lawyer sister on the West Coast, who kept pushing her to get counseling. Not her career–Army chaplain father, now stationed in Germany, who continued to urge her to get right with God. Not any of the well-intentioned acquaintances she'd left behind in Atlanta, who'd kept sending her social invitations she didn't want and coaxing her to get out and meet new people.

And the reason for her reticence?

Fear.

She'd been afraid that once she let go, once the words started to tumble out, she'd be unable to stop them. And they would reveal the dark corner of her heart where grief and rage and hate lived.

It wasn't a pretty place.

But she couldn't ignore what had just happened, either. And she'd prefer Nathan get the explanation from her rather than Zach.

She only hoped her strong feelings wouldn't turn him off.

Yet for some reason she sensed that this stranger…this man who still called her Mrs. Walker…this man with his own scars…wouldn't judge her. That he would understand.

If he didn't...if he walked away from her problem-plagued little family...she and Zach would go on together, as they had for two long years.

She'd be okay with that, she assured herself, folding her arms tight across her chest. If she could survive the loss of David, she could survive the loss of a man she hardly knew.

But it would hurt.

For reasons she didn't care to examine.

After scrubbing out every last vestige of spaghetti sauce, Nathan wrung his T-shirt out in the kitchen sink, twisting as hard as he could. The wet garment wasn't going to be comfortable—but remaining shirtless in Catherine's presence would be *less* comfortable. For both of them, he suspected.

Uneven footsteps on the stairs alerted him she was on her way down, and he worked the shirt over his head and down his chest. Then he leaned back against the kitchen counter, palms flat, fingers curled around the edge.

Wondering what was going to happen next.

She took two steps into the room and stopped, frowning. "Your shirt's wet."

"I rinsed it out. It'll dry."

"You can't wear a wet shirt. Why don't you throw it in the dryer?"

He shrugged and tried for a smile, but he only managed to coax up one side of his mouth. "I'm not accustomed to sitting in a woman's kitchen without a shirt."

"Oh." She caught her lower lip in her teeth, and he watched as uncertainty gave way to decision. "I have a shirt you can wear."

She disappeared before he could respond, and he heard her rummaging through some boxes in the front of the house. She returned with an Atlanta Braves jersey. A large one. Her husband's?

Holding it out, she gave him the glimmer of a smile when he hesitated. "Wrong team?"

"I'm okay in this, if you'd rather…if that was your husband's."

Her smile faded. "It was, a long time ago. I used it as a sleep shirt for a while. No one's worn it in years. I'm not even sure why I brought it. It has no sentimental value, if that's what you're thinking."

He *had* been thinking that. Until she'd mentioned she'd slept in it.

Clearing his throat, he leaned forward and took it from her. "Okay." After turning his back, he stripped off the T-shirt, slipped the jersey over his head and wadded his own shirt into a ball.

"Why don't you let me throw that in the dryer? By the time you leave, it will be ready to put back on." She took a step toward him and held out her hand.

He gave her the glob of damp fabric. "Thanks."

She disappeared again, through another door off the kitchen, and a few seconds later he heard the distinctive sound of a dryer at work.

When she reappeared, she hovered near the door. Tucking her hair behind her ear, she clasped her hands in front of her and shifted from one foot to the other. "Would you like to sit?"

She was nervous. Really nervous. Because he was in her kitchen again? Or because she didn't want to explain the incident with Zach?

Probably both.

It had been a long time since he'd had any occasion to practice social graces. Longer still since he'd dealt with a nervous woman. But he dug deep for whatever skills might be in hibernation, hoping they thawed quickly.

Adopting a relaxed posture, he crossed the room and sat in one of the kitchen chairs. There was no sense avoiding the obvious topic, but maybe he could lead into it.

"Will Zach be okay?"

She took the chair on the opposite side of the small table, keeping the expanse of oak between them. Resting her hands on top, she folded them into a tight knot and focused on her knuckles.

"He should be. He's always tired after one of these episodes, and sleep is the best thing for him.

I expect he'll be a little clingy for the next few days, though. This was a bad one."

Moistening her lips, she lifted her head and met his gaze. "I'm sure you're wondering what happened. Most kids don't freak out over spilled spaghetti sauce."

"He thought it was blood." He said the words quietly, watching her. As long as she'd given him an opening, why pretend he hadn't heard Zach's comment?

"Yes. It goes back to an incident he witnessed when he was four."

Silence descended, broken only by the distant caw of a gull.

When it lengthened, Nathan spoke. "Do you want to talk about it?"

"No." She unclenched her hands and massaged the center of her forehead with the tips of her fingers. "But in light of what happened earlier, you need to hear the story. That way you'll understand if Zach isn't his usual perky self for the next few days."

She reclenched her hands and swallowed. "Every Saturday morning, my husband and Zach used to go up to the corner convenience store to buy the weekend paper and a cinnamon roll. It was a ritual they both loved. Two years ago, while they were in the store, an armed robber came in."

Her voice faltered, and Nathan caught a shimmer in her green eyes. He wanted to reach over and cover her clasped fingers with his own. But he resisted, afraid she would be offended—or spooked—by the gesture.

"One of the other customers later said David turned to tuck Zach behind him. To protect him. The robber claimed he thought David was intending to rush him. To try and stop him." Her words were shakier now. But he also heard a hard undercurrent of anger. "So he shot my husband in the chest. Twice. Then he ran off while David bled to death on the floor and Zach watched."

The air whooshed out of Nathan's lungs and his stomach contorted as her stark words sank in. No wonder Zach had freaked out at the sight of spaghetti sauce all over his new friend's chest. No wonder Catherine was so protective of her son. No wonder she was wary around strangers.

He saw her bottom lip quiver. Watched as she dropped her chin and closed her eyes. Heard her suck in a harsh breath.

"I don't know what to say." He wasn't a word man. Never had been. And he'd never cared about that deficiency—until this moment. Heart aching, he wished he could dredge up some sentiment that would console this traumatized woman. "Sorry doesn't come close to capturing how badly I feel for your loss." It was the best he could do.

"Thank you." She kept her head down. Took another breath. When at last she looked up, she seemed more in control. "Don't worry. I'm not going to cry. I decided long ago that tears wouldn't change anything."

He wanted to tell her it was okay to weep over such a loss, but he didn't know her well enough to offer that kind of advice. So he stayed with the facts.

"Does this kind of thing with Zach happen often?"

"Not anymore. He hasn't retained much memory of the actual incident. But he has a vivid emotional memory, according to the child psychologist I took him to for a year. Meaning the sight of blood can trigger a very strong response. In the beginning, even a cut finger could set him off. Now, it takes a lot of blood—or what he thinks is blood—to produce an extreme reaction like he had today."

Nathan folded his own hands on top of the table. "Did they catch the guy who shot your husband?"

Her eyes hardened, the green irises chilling to the color of jade. "Yes. Within thirty minutes. He's in prison now, and if I have anything to say about it, he'll stay there for the rest of his life."

She shoved back her chair with enough force to startle Nathan, then rose to pace the room despite her limp, her posture taut, the planes of her face sharp with agitation. "I'll never forget sitting at his trial, listening to the defense attorney try to excuse his behavior and make a case for a reduced sentence. He'd come from an impoverished background. He was raised in a broken home. The system had failed him by not recognizing the need to remove him from a dysfunctional environment. He got in with a bad crowd. It was society's fault." Sarcasm dripped from her words as she mimicked the arguments that had been put forth.

Swinging toward him, she gripped the back of a chair, her eyes flashing with anger—and another emotion that was all too familiar to him.

Hate.

"The sympathy card didn't work with me. When I looked at that creep who exhibited not one single shred of human decency, who never once expressed an iota of regret for what he'd done, I didn't see a victim. I saw a killer. A violent criminal who got exactly what he deserved. I hope he rots in prison for the rest of his life. Along with all the other malicious felons who don't deserve any more consideration than they gave their victims."

As Catherine's merciless assessment quivered in

the air between them, Nathan tried to breathe. Tried to keep his stomach from curdling. Tried to distance himself from her tirade.

But he couldn't.

Because his participation in the armed robbery of a convenience store was what had put him behind bars for ten years.

No one had been killed in that incident. But they could have been. He and Trace had both been nervous. If someone had tried to stop them, he didn't think his partner in crime would have hesitated to use his gun. In the heat of the moment, as his own panic and self-preservation instincts kicked in, he might have, too. And in the process, he might have snuffed out the life of a good man like David Walker.

That was the harsh truth of it.

Meaning he was no better than the man Catherine hated.

As the silence between them lengthened, her knuckles whitened on the back of the chair and her chin tipped up. "I'm sorry if that sounds callous. But it's how I feel."

"I can understand your bitterness." Somehow he got the hoarse words past his choked throat.

Her eyes narrowed a fraction, and he could feel the tension vibrating in her body. "My father thinks I'll never find peace until I forgive the man who killed my husband. But he doesn't have to deal with a traumatized child. Nor did he lose the partner he loved. When I asked him how a caring God could let such a thing happen, he didn't have an answer that made sense to me. And he's a minister."

"Sometimes it's hard to understand God's ways."

"No kidding." She gave a derisive snort.

"I didn't think He cared, either, until two years ago." The revelation came out before he could stop it, catching him off guard. He didn't talk much about his newfound faith. A lot of his fellow inmates had ribbed him about it, and he'd learned to keep this thoughts to himself. His cherished relationship with the Lord had been fragile in the beginning, and he'd done his best to protect it. Nurture it.

But it was strong enough now to withstand ridicule and attack. And somehow he sensed Catherine could benefit from hearing a little piece of his story. "Some bad things had happened to me, too, and I was angry at Him—and the world."

Her grip on the chair eased a fraction. "What changed your mind?"

"Love." It might not be the profound answer she'd been looking for, but it was the truth. "I finally opened myself to love from my siblings—

and from God. It changed my life—and taught me that despite the bad stuff, goodness does exists as a strong, sustaining force that casts light into the darkest places. It also taught me how to forgive."

Quiet descended in the room, Catherine apparently as surprised as he was by his unexpected eloquence.

As she straightened up, there was a soul-deep sadness in her eyes—and resignation in their depths. "You're a better person than I am, that's all I can say."

"No." His dissent was swift. "That's not true. In spite of a terrible tragedy, you're doing a good job with Zach. And you're creating a new life for the two of you. That takes strength—and a lot of courage."

Once more, he caught a suspicious sheen in her eyes before she turned away. "It doesn't take courage to do what you have to do. And any strength you think you see is an illusion." She pulled open the freezer and buried her head in the icy depths. "If you want to wash up, I'll put the pizza in the oven. Zach won't sleep long."

Taking the cue, he rose and pushed through the back door. And as he headed to the sink in the guest quarters where he always cleaned up, he mulled over the dilemma he now faced.

He had hoped coming to Nantucket would give

him a fresh start. One unencumbered by his checkered history. J.C. and Marci had both encouraged him to leave the past behind after he was released from prison, to focus on the future. And they'd done everything they could to help him. They'd offered moral support. They'd rented Edith's cottage for him for the entire summer to help smooth his transition back to the civilian world and give him a chance to figure out what he wanted to do with the rest of his life. They'd even plied him with art supplies.

But maybe it had been a pipe dream to think he could start over with a blank canvas, he conceded, a pang echoing in his heart as he sudsed his hands. Maybe he'd never be able to wash away the taint of his mistakes. Sooner or later, people would learn about his record. He'd hoped it would be later, after he'd established some credibility and trust in the community. But if other residents felt even half as strongly about people with criminal pasts as Catherine did, he was doomed.

Grabbing a towel, he dried his hands and debated his next move. Should he keep his secret for now, hoping that in time his friendship with her might grow to the point where his past was less important? Or should he be upfront and put the outcome in God's hands?

No answer came to him as he hung the towel

back on the rack and stepped into the room he'd transformed over the past five days. Maybe he should sleep on the decision. And pray for guidance.

Opting for that plan, he headed back to the house to eat pizza.

And hoped it didn't get stuck in his throat.

"That was good, Mrs. Walker. Thank you for inviting me."

As Nathan wiped his lips on a paper napkin and crumbled it into a ball, Catherine examined his plate. Half of one of the two pieces of pizza he'd taken remained.

The episode with Zach must have killed his appetite. And her angry tirade hadn't helped. She hadn't meant to rant about the man who'd taken David's life. But as she'd feared, once she'd opened the floodgates, her fury had poured through.

Unfortunately, her intuition that this man, too, had endured heartache and would understand her feelings appeared to have been off base. Since he'd returned from the guest quarters, he'd distanced himself. An almost tangible tension crackled in the air.

Stifling a surge of disappointment, she attempted to restore the easy give and take that had begun to develop between them. "I'm glad you stayed for dinner. And let's make it Catherine. I think we've moved past the *Mrs.* stage, don't you?"

Zach spoke up before he could respond. "Do we have any cookies, Mom?"

"I think I can round up a few." She rose and walked to the pantry. "Would you like some coffee, Nathan?"

"No." He stood, too. "I need to be going."

"Already?" Zach gave him a disappointed look.

"It's way past quitting time, champ." Nathan leaned over and tousled Zach's hair. "And I have things to do tonight."

"Like what?"

"Zach. That's Nathan's private business." Catherine withdrew a package of vanilla sandwich cookies and set them on the table. "Let me get your shirt." She walked over to the laundry room, pulled it from the dryer, and handed it to him. "We'll see you Monday, then?" He was hovering at the screen door, as if he couldn't wait to get away.

"Yes." Turning aside, he stripped off the jersey and slipped on the T-shirt in one smooth motion. Handing the jersey back to her, he lifted a hand toward Zach. "See you later, champ."

"'Bye, Nathan."

With a nod to her, he pushed through the screen

door, crossed the breezeway in a few long strides and disappeared around the front of the house.

Leaving her to wonder if she'd ever see him again.

For despite his reassurance that he'd be back Monday, despite the fact that he didn't strike her as the kind of man who would walk out on a job or renege on a commitment, she didn't like the vibes she'd picked up during their pizza dinner.

But if he did decide to quit…if he exited her life as unexpectedly as he'd entered it…she'd find someone to step in and take Nathan's place.

On the project, if not in her heart.

For even in their short acquaintance, he'd managed to awaken a tenderness that had long lain dormant—connecting with her just as he'd connected with Zach.

If he left, her son would miss him. A lot.

And so would she.

Chapter Five

Nathan braked to a stop in front of Catherine's house on Saturday, swung his leg over the bar on the bike, set the kickstand…and tried to fight down the worst case of nerves he'd suffered since he'd stood in the courtroom waiting for his sentence to be read.

The outcome that day hadn't been good.

And he wasn't confident it would be any better this morning.

But after a night spent tossing and turning, he'd realized his only ethical choice was to tell Catherine about his background. Keeping it secret wasn't an option he could live with in good conscience.

And if she sent him away…

The roiling in his stomach told him that was a very real possibility, given the strength of her feelings about the man who had killed her husband—and about felons in general.

Mustering his courage, he started up the gravel path to the front door—only to halt a moment later at the unexpected sound of violin music.

He didn't recognize the piece. But each pure, clear note of the poignant melody throbbed with feeling as it hung suspended in the hushed morning air. Unlike the uplifting music the string quartet had played at Marci's wedding, however, this composition spoke of aching sadness. Of a yearning for things that could never be. Of remembered joy that was long past.

Nathan could picture Catherine as she played: eyes closed, head tipped into the chin rest, right hand masterfully wielding the bow as the fingertips of her left hand caressed the strings. She would be swaying slightly, lost in the magic of the music.

The way she'd been at Marci's wedding.

He was no musician, but Nathan knew he was listening to a master. To a woman who had not only technical expertise, but the ability to imbue her music with a passion that could touch listeners' hearts and stir their souls while offering a glimpse into her own.

"Nathan?"

The childish voice broke the spell. Spotting Zach at a window, he lifted his hand in greeting.

"Hey, Mom!" The little boy's volume doubled. As did his enthusiasm. "Nathan's here!"

The music stopped abruptly.

As the youngster disappeared, Nathan resumed his trek toward the front door. Catherine opened it when he was halfway up the steps, looking as surprised as her son.

"Nathan…I didn't expect you until Monday." The faint shadows under her eyes suggested sleep had been as elusive for her as it had been for him.

"I had something I wanted to talk over with you. Is this a bad time?"

"No. Not at all. I'm playing at a wedding later, but I don't have to leave for a couple of hours. Come in."

She pushed the door open, and he stepped inside.

Withdrawing a DVD from the inside pocket of his jean jacket, he smiled at Zach as he handed it over. "Remember that movie I mentioned last week? The one about the boys who built rockets? I found a copy for you."

"Awesome!" Zach examined the cover and looked up at Catherine. "Can I watch it now, Mom? Please?"

"It's PG," Nathan assured her over Zach's head. "I thought it would occupy him while we talked."

Her uncertain gaze met his, and he saw a flicker of distress in her green eyes. "Sure. I'll get it started for you, Zach." She took the DVD and motioned Nathan toward the kitchen. "I'll meet you out there in a minute."

With a nod, Nathan headed toward the back of the house, trying to quiet the thudding of his heart. And hoping Catherine would be able to see beyond his criminal record to the man he'd become. To understand that the street thug he'd once been didn't exist anymore.

If she couldn't, he'd lose this job.

He'd also lose his connection—tenuous though it was—to her and Zach.

And much as he wanted this job, the loss of the latter would be even worse.

Catherine fiddled with the DVD far longer than necessary, buying herself a few minutes to think through Nathan's unexpected appearance. And come to the obvious conclusion.

He was going to quit—just as she'd feared yesterday when he'd left.

She couldn't blame him, either. Why would he want to work for a bitter, angry, aloof woman when there were plenty of other jobs on the island? Closer to town, too. After all, she hadn't given him the warmest reception. From the moment she'd seen him at that wedding, she'd made no attempt to mask her wariness. He must think...

"Come on, Mom. It's not hard. Do you want me to do it?"

At Zach's impatient query, Catherine cranked up

the volume a little higher than usual, pushed the play button and set the remote on top of the TV.

"I'll be in the kitchen with Nathan."

"Okay." Already his focus was on the screen.

Wiping her palms on her jeans, she limped toward the back of the house.

Nathan was leaning against the counter, hands in his pockets. The tense line of his shoulders was at odds with his casual stance, setting off another flutter in her stomach.

"Would you like some coffee?"

"Sure."

She busied herself at the pot. After filling two mugs, she retrieved the pitcher of cream from the fridge and set it on the table.

"I heard you playing the violin when I arrived." Nathan broke the heavy silence. "You have an incredible talent."

"I've been at it a long time. I played with the Atlanta Philharmonic for a lot of years, plus with a string quartet. I thought I'd have difficulty finding opportunities here, but it turned out that Becky—the real estate agent I used—is also a musician. She plays the viola. Anyway, she's part of a string quartet, and their violinist just moved to the mainland. So when she found out about my background, she invited me to play with them. It should work out great."

Stop babbling, Catherine berated herself as she set the mugs on the table. *The man has something to say. Let him get to it. Delaying the inevitable isn't going to change anything.*

"Sorry." She took a seat and gestured to an empty chair. "You didn't come all the way out here on your day off to listen to a boring recitation of my musical résumé."

He took the chair she'd indicated and wrapped his hands around his mug. "I'm not bored. I'm happy you found an outlet for your art." He took a sip of coffee. "How's Zach doing?"

"Okay. He didn't even have a nightmare last night, like he sometimes does after an episode. That's an encouraging sign."

"Good." He set his mug on the table, never breaking eye contact. "I thought a lot about the story you told me yesterday, Catherine."

He'd called her Catherine. That was a positive. Wasn't it?

"I shouldn't have dumped the whole thing on you at once like that." She sent him an apologetic look. "And I'm sorry I got so angry. I've kept my feelings bottled inside for a long time, and I'm afraid they came out very strong."

"You were honest. I respect that. And you deserve honesty in return."

Her heart skipped a beat. "You're quitting, aren't

you?" The impulsive words were out before she could stop them.

He blinked at her, then frowned. "Why would you think that?"

She toyed with her mug, staring into the dark depths of her coffee. "I'm sure there are friendlier people to work for. I haven't exactly welcomed you with open arms. Or gone out of my way to be nice."

Nathan shook his head and raked his fingers through his hair, his expression unreadable. "You have legitimate reasons for being cautious, Catherine. As for friendliness—I haven't felt unwelcome since you hired me. I didn't come here to quit because of what you told me, either. But you may *want* me to quit after you hear what I have to say."

Now it was her turn to frown. "What do you mean?"

Once more he gripped his mug with both hands. "You didn't ask about my background when I applied for the job."

"You came recommended by a doctor, and you've done jobs for one of the local ministers. That sufficed as a reference for me. And I've seen your work. It's excellent. You're fast, thorough and conscientious. What more do I need to know?"

"Plenty."

The grim line of his mouth put her on alert, even

as she fought the surprisingly strong urge to reach over and smooth away the furrows etched on his brow. To tell him to relax. Instead, she sat watching…and waiting.

He took a sip of coffee, then set the mug aside and folded his hands on the table, his gaze steady. "I'd like to go way back to the beginning of the story, if you'll humor me for a few minutes. I'll try to keep it as short as I can."

"Okay."

"My brother and sister and I grew up in a very blue-collar family that could, at best, be called dysfunctional. From the time I was seven, I was a very angry, messed-up kid. When I was thirteen, my dad deserted us. After that, my mom worked two jobs to try and make ends meet. Our neighborhood was rough, and with her gone so much, I got in with the wrong crowd. My older brother, J.C.— he's a detective now on the island—did his best to keep me out of trouble, but it was a losing battle. Especially after my mom was killed two years later in a hit-and-run accident."

Although his tone was dispassionate, Catherine saw a flicker of pain—and regret—in his eyes. A sudden tingle in her nerve endings warned her she wasn't going to like what he was about to tell her.

"You've seen the scar on my chest, Catherine. It's from a knife wound I got in a street fight." He gentled his voice, as if he hoped that might soften the harsh facts.

It didn't. Shock rippled through her.

"I'm sure you've noticed the ones on my face, too. Also the result of fights. The day I applied for this job, Zach asked how I'd broken my fingers. I didn't answer then, but I will now. A police officer's baton smashed them."

She cringed—an involuntary reaction she wished she could recall when a muscle in his jaw twitched. But he kept going, his expression stoic.

"I got deeper and deeper into trouble, Catherine. J.C. tried to help me. So did my sister, Marci, in the beginning. I pushed them both away and dropped out of school at sixteen. For the next eight years I lived a life I wish I could erase from my biography. Meanwhile, J.C. became a cop. He warned me my luck would eventually run out.

"One day, it did. A buddy convinced me to rob a convenience store. With guns. We'd done our share of shoplifting, everything from electronics to jewelry, but this was big-time stuff. I wasn't gung ho on the idea, but he persuaded me we could pull it off. Except we didn't count on the clerk tripping the silent alarm. The next thing we knew, the place was surrounded by police."

His Adam's apple bobbed. "I'll skip all the court stuff and cut to the chase. I was convicted of armed robbery and served ten years in prison. I was released less than a month ago—a few days before Marci's wedding."

Silence fell in the room as Catherine tried to process all Nathan had told her.

He'd robbed a store with a gun. Aimed it at innocent bystanders like David. Might have pulled the trigger if he'd been provoked.

Meaning he could have committed murder.

A shudder ran through her, and she closed her eyes as the full impact of Nathan's story registered.

A convicted felon—a man just like the criminal who'd killed her husband—was sitting in her kitchen.

Except…somehow she couldn't reconcile the Nathan Clay at her table with the angry, hostile punk he'd described.

It didn't compute.

Opening her eyes, she stared at the man across from her. He hadn't moved a muscle. His hands were still folded in front of him. But the creases at the corners of his eyes seemed deeper. And grooves had appeared beside his mouth.

She tried to find her voice. When she did, her words came out faint and scratchy. "That's quite a story."

He leaned forward. "There's more. The best

part. Two years ago, thanks to J.C.'s and Marci's love and the grace of God, I turned a corner. I asked for forgiveness, and I started over. I finished high school. I developed a relationship with my family and with the Lord. I resolved that I wasn't going to let my dark past keep me from having a bright future. I'm not the same man I was ten years ago, Catherine. People *can* change. If they want to."

Not hardened criminals.

The automatic denial echoed in Catherine's mind. As it had been doing for the past two years.

Yet…Nathan claimed to have changed dramatically. *Had* changed dramatically, if his description of his younger days was accurate.

Didn't that mean, though, that the man who'd killed David could change, too?

That maybe he already had?

Catherine thought about the letter that had arrived from him, via his attorney, a few months ago. The cover note had simply said his client had asked him to pass it on.

She hadn't even unfolded the single sheet of paper. Instead, she'd torn it into tiny pieces and thrown it in the fireplace, watching the flames destroy it as his crime had destroyed her world.

It didn't matter what he had to say, she'd told herself as she'd watched the fire consume the fragments. No apology, no remorse, would bring David back or restore the life they'd shared. Her husband's killer didn't deserve her compassion—or her forgiveness. Because criminals didn't change.

Now, for the first time, a flicker of doubt seeped into her mind.

"Catherine?"

At Nathan's quiet prod, she looked at him.

"All I'm asking for is a chance."

To do what? Shake her resolve? Undermine her convictions? Take away the consuming hate and bitterness that had allowed her to keep other debilitating emotions—like grief—at bay?

She couldn't let that happen. She'd fall apart.

Rising abruptly, she put as much distance as possible between them, wedging herself into the far corner of the kitchen next to the counter.

"Why didn't you tell me this sooner?" The words came out cold. Accusatory.

"I haven't shared my past with anyone here. I didn't want to be judged based on who I was, but on who I am. Maybe that was too much to hope for." His tone was quiet. Resigned. He rose and faced her. "Do I still have a job here?"

His rigid posture suggested he had braced himself for her answer. Only she didn't have one. "I don't know. I...I need to think about it."

There was a hint of defeat in his eyes as he gave a stiff nod. "Is it okay if I say goodbye to Zach?"

"Yes."

He moved back into the hall and headed toward the living room. She trailed behind, maintaining a safe distance.

Safe from what, she wasn't certain.

He paused on the threshold of the living room, which was still cluttered with boxes. Zach, wedged into an empty corner of the sofa, was absorbed in the drama unfolding on the screen.

"'Bye, champ."

Her son flashed Nathan a grin. "'Bye, Nathan. I'll help you paint next week, okay?"

"Whatever your mom says." When he looked at her, Catherine tried not to let the hurt in his deep-brown eyes touch her soul. He was practically a stranger, after all. It was crazy to feel such angst over a man she hadn't even known two weeks ago.

"You'll be in touch?"

At his quiet question, she nodded. "Yes. By tomorrow."

"Okay." He opened the door and turned. "Goodbye, Catherine."

He said it like he didn't think he'd be coming back.

Pulling the door shut behind him, he secured it with a soft click.

For a full minute, Catherine stood unmoving in the hall, struggling with the irony of it all. Yesterday, she'd been afraid *he* might ditch the job for one with a boss who had fewer issues.

Now he seemed to be thinking she'd ditch him.

And maybe she would.

Because his presence day after day could play havoc with her once-a-bad-apple, always-a-bad-apple view of the man who'd killed her husband. A view that gave her an excuse to hold on to hate, discount the notion of forgiveness—and keep grief at arm's length. A view that allowed her to survive.

Catherine saw no reason to disrupt her world again. She was doing okay the way she was. Getting through the days. Holding on. Not gracefully, perhaps, but at least she hadn't plummeted into the black pit she'd been dangling over for the past two years.

If her grip slipped, though…if she started to fall…she was doomed. There was no one to catch her. To save her from the dark abyss.

And she didn't think she could take that risk.

Chapter Six

Checking the address on the slip of paper in his hand, Nathan turned onto India Street.

Home of the Blue Water Gallery.

As he juggled the two canvases in his arms, a barrage of serious second thoughts overwhelmed him, and his step faltered. This was crazy. He had no more business showing his work to a high-end gallery owner than he had hoping people could overlook his seedy past.

Tightening his jaw, he fought back a wave of despair. Okay, so things with Catherine hadn't gone as he'd hoped this morning. But he still had a job. She hadn't told him to get lost, had she?

Only because she was blindsided. She didn't have time to think through everything you said. Once she does, you're out of there.

He tried to ignore the pessimistic voice in his

head, but he had a feeling it spoke the truth. That before the weekend was over, she'd let him go.

With that disheartening probability weighing on his mind, he'd decided to follow up on Kate Mac-Donald's suggestion to visit the gallery owner who'd handled her husband's work. Maybe the woman would offer him some encouragement that would brighten his dismal mood.

In truth, though, he doubted his odds on that score were any better than they were with Catherine.

As he approached the gallery, Nathan surveyed the clapboard structure. Painted Federal blue, with white trim around the windows, it looked as if it had once been a house. A discreet sign identifying it as the Blue Water Gallery hung from an iron rod on one side of the door.

For two full minutes, Nathan stood in front, trying to gather up his courage. But after a passing group of noisy tourists jostled him on the uneven brick sidewalk and he almost lost his grip on the paintings, he opened the door and crossed the threshold.

And felt as if he'd stepped into another world.

Here, quiet reigned. There were no crowds, no clutter. Just open space. The hardwood floor had been buffed to a satin finish, and the soft white walls offered a perfect backdrop for the artwork that had been framed and lit to display it to its best advantage.

Two rooms opened off the foyer, and the center of each held three-dimensional art—a bronze sculpture in one, a display of glass bowls in the other.

The place reeked of class. And talent. And money.

In other words, he was way out of his league.

Losing his nerve, Nathan headed for the door.

"May I help you?"

At the sound of a female voice, he stopped and closed his eyes. Too late to escape unnoticed. But he'd think of some excuse to get out of here. Save himself the embarrassment of having the owner tell him his work stunk.

He turned. A woman, as tall as he was, wearing a black pants ensemble brightened at the neck with a colorful scarf, gave him a pleasant smile. Based on the touches of gray in her darkbrown hair, he guessed she was in her early to midfifties.

"I was just looking around."

"I'm glad you stopped in." She moved forward and extended her hand. "I'm the owner, Monica Stevens."

He had to set the paintings down in order to return her greeting, and as she gave him a firm shake, her gaze flickered to them. "Those look like pieces of art."

"That term might be a little too generous." He rubbed his palms on his jeans, knowing he was stuck. "I'm Nathan Clay. I understand you represented the work of Kate MacDonald's husband. She saw one of my paintings and thought you might be interested in it. I believe she was going to call you."

The woman's smile broadened. "Yes, she did. I've been hoping you'd stop by. She spoke very highly of the piece she saw, and I'm always looking for new talent."

He picked up the paintings again. "I don't know about the talent part. I haven't had any training, and I'm new to painting. Mostly I've done sketches."

"Did you bring some of those, too?"

"Yes." At the last minute, he'd tucked one of his notebooks from prison in between the two paintings. "But they're rough. Not saleable material. I just thought they might help you evaluate my abilities."

"Let's take a look."

She led the way toward the back of the building, to a small room containing various pieces of art not yet on display. Adjusting the lighting, she gestured toward a workbench in the middle of the room. "You can set them there."

Nathan had put only a single layer of brown paper around the canvases, but his hands fumbled as he removed it. When at last they were free, he arranged them on the workbench, set his notebook beside them and stepped back.

Slipping on a pair of tortoiseshell glasses, Monica studied first one painting, then the other, as they lay flat on the bench. She didn't rush. She didn't speak. She just looked.

Nathan felt a bead of sweat form between his shoulder blades. Slowly it trickled down his back under his cotton shirt.

Finally she reached for the painting of the little boy on the beach. The one Edith and Kate had admired. Angling it this way and that, she inspected it in different lights.

When she finished with that one, she picked up his second effort. It was another beach scene, and again it featured a little boy. But this child was dark-haired and much farther in the distance. Ominous clouds were gathering on the horizon behind him. He was alone on the vast stretch of shoreline, and seemed oblivious to the approaching storm as he carried a bucket of water from the ocean toward a hole he'd dug in the sand.

"Two very different moods." Monica's murmured comment didn't seem to require a response, and Nathan remained silent.

At last she turned, the second painting still in her hands as she scrutinized him. "These pieces represent an interesting dichotomy. Anyone would find that one appealing." She gestured toward the happy child whose face was lifted toward the heavens. "But it will take a customer with a discerning eye to appreciate the depth of this one. And the layers."

Once more she examined the painting in her hands. Then she set it aside and opened his notebook.

Nathan had no idea how long he stood in silence as she perused his drawings. But it felt like an hour. She took her time with every one, asking no questions, making no comments.

He had no idea what she thought.

Reaching the end of the notebook, she closed it, turned to him and removed her glasses.

"You have an amazing talent. The compassion and depth of feeling in your work is remarkable."

The stiffness went out of his legs, and he grasped the edge of the workbench to steady himself. "Thank you."

"I'd like to represent these paintings if you're interested in selling them."

"Yes. Thank you." She liked his work. Enough to display it in this high-class gallery.

It was mind blowing.

"I charge a forty percent commission on the sale price for all of the artists I represent. Is that acceptable?"

"Yes."

"I'll mail you some paperwork to sign, but in the meantime I'd like to go ahead and frame these for display. Is that all right with you?"

"Yes." He knew he was beginning to sound like a parrot, but he couldn't manage to formulate more than a word or two at once.

"As for pricing..." She pursed her lips and studied the paintings again. "I think I can get more for that one, with the right buyer." She gestured to the one with dark clouds, then named two dollar amounts. "How does that sound?"

Nathan hoped his eyes weren't bugging out of his head. He'd expected her to price them at a fraction of what she'd quoted—if she took them at all.

She smiled. "You seem surprised."

"I am." He shoved his hands into his pockets. "It's hard to believe anyone would part with that much money for a piece by an unknown artist."

"My clientele is always hoping to discover the next star. Art is an investment for them. Sometimes their investments pay off, sometimes they don't." She surveyed Nathan's work again. "I have a strong feeling this one will. I sense tremendous potential here, and my instincts rarely fail me." She held out her hand again. "Do we have a deal?"

"Yes." He took it and gave a firm shake.

Five minutes later, as he headed back down

India Street toward Lighthouse Lane, his heart felt lighter—and more hopeful.

If Monica Stevens could see the potential—and compassion—in his art, maybe, just maybe, Catherine would see the potential and compassion in his *heart*.

"How come we don't go to church anymore?" Zach stood beside Catherine as she flipped pancakes on Sunday morning, staying closer than usual—as he'd been doing since Friday's spaghetti sauce incident. Except when he'd watched the movie Nathan brought yesterday, he'd barely let her out of his sight.

"We just moved here and we've been busy. Then I broke my toes, so I'm not going anywhere right now." It was a poor excuse, and she knew it.

So did Zach. "I thought you said you were going to the grocery store tomorrow?"

"That's tomorrow, not today." She began sliding the spatula under the pancakes and piling them onto two plates. "Can you get the butter out for me?"

He ambled toward the fridge. "I miss Sunday school."

"I know, honey. We'll go back to church again soon."

Even though her heart hadn't been in it, she'd continued to take Zach to services in Atlanta after

David died. As a minister's kid, she had the Sunday ritual embedded in her DNA. Besides, she knew David would have wanted her to raise Zach with a solid grounding in faith. She'd get around to finding a church here…one of these days. For Zach's sake.

But the more pressing problem was figuring out how to break the news to him that she was going to let Nathan go.

It hadn't been an easy decision. She'd spent a sleepless night wrestling with it. But in the end, she'd come to the conclusion that to preserve her peace of mind, it was her only option. Having Nathan around disturbed her—and rocked her world—on way too many levels.

She'd come up with a different explanation for Zach, however. One she hoped he'd accept.

"Can I stay here with Nathan tomorrow when you go to the grocery store?"

He'd given her the perfect opening for the discussion they needed to have. Ready or not.

Not being the operative word.

Catherine set their plates on the table, tried to psych herself up for the coming exchange and motioned Zach into his chair. "I want to talk to you about Nathan."

Some of the color left her son's face. "He's okay, isn't he?"

"Yes, honey, he's fine." She reached over and laid her hand on top of his for a moment, then buttered his pancakes as she continued. "You saw him yesterday, remember?"

"Yeah." He ran his finger through a stream of melting butter and licked it. "So why do you want to talk about him?"

"Well, there are a lot of other people who need help with their house projects, like we did." She began cutting up his pancakes. "And Nathan's a good worker, isn't he?"

"Yeah." Zach speared a bite and stuck it in his mouth.

"So he's going to be helping some of those other people from now on."

Zach stopped chewing. "You mean, he's not coming back?"

"No, honey."

"But he isn't finished. Who's gonna do the rest of the work?"

"I'm going to do some. And I'll get someone else to help a little for another week or two."

"Why can't those other people wait until Nathan is done here?"

Catherine pushed her cooling pancakes around on her plate. She should have known Zach wouldn't accept her flawed explanation. Her son had inherited David's keen sense of logic.

Since she had nothing better to offer, she resorted to the old it's-this-way-because-I-say-so response. "That's just how it is, Zach. Eat your pancakes before they get cold."

He jabbed one with his fork, his expression forlorn. "I'm not hungry anymore."

Neither was she.

A full minute passed while they both pushed the food around their plates.

"Doesn't he like us anymore, Mom?"

Zach's small, uncertain voice tore at her heart, and she folded his hand in hers. "He likes us a lot, honey. He especially liked how much you helped him. But he wasn't going to stay forever anyway, you know. As soon as he finished our work, he would have gone on to another job."

"Does that mean we won't ever see him again? Like we never saw Daddy again?"

Catherine's stomach twisted into a knot. "Daddy went to heaven, Zach. Nathan is still here. We might see him again."

He chased a slippery square of butter around his plate with his fork. "I hope so. He's really nice, Mom. It was happier when he was here."

She couldn't dispute that.

"But we have each other." She summoned up a smile. "So we'll be fine. Right?"

He didn't answer. And she didn't push.

Because she had a feeling his response would mirror the doubt in her own heart.

The quiet buzz in his pocket threw Nathan for a moment—until he remembered he'd put his phone on vibrate during the Sunday service and had forgotten to reset it to audible.

Pulling it out, he had to search for the talk button on the bare-bones, pay-by-the-minute throwaway that was sufficient for his limited needs. In general, Marci and J.C. were the only people who called him, and since J.C. lived next door, he was more likely to stop by than use the phone, anyway. Nathan had loaded it with sixty minutes of air time, and he doubted he'd used more than ten of them in the three weeks he'd been on the island.

As he put the phone to his ear, his pulse kicked up a notch. He'd seen J.C. and Marci at church less than an hour ago, meaning there was little chance either of them would be calling him.

It must be Catherine.

His assumption was verified as she greeted him, the slight southern accent in her contralto voice instantly recognizable. Under other circumstances, he would have enjoyed listening to it. But today she sounded nervous.

Not a good sign.

"Do you have a minute to talk?"

Sitting in one of the chairs at the small café table in the tiny kitchenette of Edith's rental cottage, he braced himself. "Yes."

"I promised I'd get back to you about the project. You've done a great job, Nathan, so this has nothing to do with your work. But I have a lot of baggage, as you discovered Friday. And the thing is, your background is so similar to…well, I don't think I can get past it. It might be better if I find someone else to finish the job."

Her decision wasn't unexpected. He'd seen her look of horror as he'd recounted his history. But it hurt nonetheless.

"I understand."

"Is it okay if I mail you a check?"

She didn't even want him stopping by to pick it up. His spirits took another nosedive.

"Sure. You can send it to me in care of The Devon Rose." He recited the address. "Listen…tell Zach he's still my buddy, okay?" His voice rasped on the last word, and he cleared his throat.

"I will. Thanks for all your hard work."

"It was my pleasure."

"Goodbye, Nathan."

The line went dead.

Punching the end button, he set the phone on the table and tried not to take the rejection personally. His failure to convince Catherine to overlook his past was more a reflection of her own history than of his, he told himself. Others with less trauma in their pasts might be better able to judge him on his current merits.

But even if that was true, he was going to miss the lovely violinist and her charming son.

A lot.

Resting his elbows on the small table, Nathan steepled his fingers and tried to lift his spirits by reminding himself how blessed he was. This cottage was a good example. None of the other guys he'd done time with had traded a cell for digs like this, courtesy of a brother and sister who loved him.

The unaccustomed luxury had actually thrown him in the beginning. When Marci and J.C. had ushered him in, he'd been stunned by the marked contrast not only to his prison quarters, but to any of his preincarceration abodes. For the first few days, he'd been afraid to touch anything.

He was more comfortable and relaxed now, but he never failed to appreciate—and relish—the bright, airy decor. Though the place was small by most people's standards, the vaulted ceiling gave an illusion of spaciousness. A queen-size bed stood on the polished pine floor in one corner, while a sitting area boasted a small couch upholstered in floral fabric. A brass reading lamp stood beside it, and an old chest, topped with a glass bowl of hard candy, served as a coffee table. A kitchenette and private bath completed the floor plan. It was more room than he'd ever had all to himself. And best of all, there were no bars. Anywhere.

What more could a guy ask for?

A family to love.

As that answer echoed through his mind, an image of Catherine and Zach followed close on its heels.

And the ache returned to his heart.

Nathan had always known the odds of connecting with the first woman to catch his eye were miniscule. He'd acknowledged that very thing at Marci's wedding, when he'd first noticed the lovely violin player.

But why couldn't the odds, for once, have been in his favor?

Lost in thought—and wallowing in a healthy dose of self-pity—he missed the first knock on his door. But he heard the second one. Loud and clear. Checking his watch, he was surprised to discover twenty minutes had passed since Catherine's call.

When he opened the door, he found his brother on the other side.

"I thought you were going to meet us at the garage?" J.C. raised an eyebrow.

Brunch. He'd agreed to go with J.C. and Heather

to brunch. The commitment had totally slipped his mind after Catherine's call.

"I'm sorry. I got distracted."

"Yeah? Well, I'll let you explain that to Heather. She's starving. At his stage of her pregnancy, mealtime is sacrosanct. Anybody who messes with it does so at his own risk."

The shadow of a smile tugged at Nathan's lips. "Apologize for me, okay?"

"No way. It's your neck on the line, buddy."

"Look, J.C., if you don't mind, I think I'll pass today."

His big brother frowned. "How come? You were all set to go when we drove home from church."

"I'm just not in the mood anymore."

J.C. folded his arms across his chest and squinted at him. At six-foot-one, with dark hair and penetrating brown eyes, Detective Cole was a force to be reckoned with. Nathan doubted much got past his brother on the job.

Or off.

"What changed your mood during the past forty-five minutes?"

"It's not important, J.C."

"It is to me."

Those four words said it all, Nathan reflected. The visits J.C. had made to the prison, and the letters he'd continued to write—even after Nathan had refused to talk to him year after year—had eloquently communicated his love. The love that had been Nathan's salvation. That same love was J.C.'s motivation for probing today, Nathan knew. If something was bothering his kid brother, he cared enough to risk Nathan's ire to find out—and help, if he could.

Except there was nothing he could do to remedy this situation. Nathan's fate with Catherine had been sealed years ago, by his own bad choices.

But J.C. would find out soon enough he'd lost his job. There was no sense keeping it secret.

Shoving his hands into his pockets, he shrugged. "I got fired."

J.C.'s frown deepened. "I thought the job was going well."

"It was. She liked my work. But she had a hard time dealing with my past."

"I thought you weren't going to bring that up right away?"

"I wasn't. There were extenuating circumstances. I found out her husband was killed by an armed robber two years ago. In light of that, I couldn't in good conscience keep my history secret."

J.C. raked his fingers through his hair and shook his head. "What a bizarre coincidence."

"Tell me about it."

"Then this wasn't about you."

"She said as much."

"You won't have any problem finding another job. There are plenty of people on the island looking for good workers with your skills."

"I'm not worried about that. I plan to talk to Reverend Kaiser tomorrow and see if he has any leads. And I'll put up ads on a couple of the bulletin boards I've seen around town."

Heaving a sigh, J.C. propped his fists on his hips. "You remind me of Marci when she arrived. Her visit was supposed to be a vacation, too. So what did she do? She took on a massive garden restoration and then got involved in developing an elder-assistance program. Doesn't anyone in this family know how to relax?"

"What's that old saying about the pot and the kettle?"

J.C. smirked. "Very funny. But you don't have to plunge into work right away, you know. Take a few weeks to chill out. Do some more painting, now that you have a gallery interested in your work."

He'd told his siblings about yesterday's visit to the Blue Water Gallery, though he hadn't mentioned the exorbitant price Monica had put on his paintings. He doubted they'd ever sell. But he'd been thrilled by her interest. J.C. and Marci had been, too.

"I plan to. But I'll feel more comfortable if I develop a steady source of income. I'm not going to mooch off you and Marci forever."

"You're not mooching. These three months are our gift to you."

"And I appreciate it. But I want to earn some of my keep."

J.C. huffed out a breath. "You're stubborn, you know that? Just like your sister."

"Join the club."

"Ha, ha." He folded his arms across his chest and his demeanor grew more serious. "Listen, don't let this job thing get you down, okay?"

"I won't. Now go take the mother-to-be to brunch. I don't want Heather to be mad at me for delaying chow time."

"Yeah." J.C. checked his watch again. "The Devon Rose hath no fury like a hungry woman. You're sure you won't go?"

"Another time."

"All right. I'll check in later."

With a wave, J.C. strode down the stone path that led to the gate in the privet hedge around Edith's backyard.

Closing the door, Nathan tried to take J.C.'s advice to heart. Of all the jobs he could have taken on Nantucket, how ironic was it that he'd find one with a woman whose experience would predispose her to dislike him? But as his brother had also pointed out, there were plenty of other jobs out there.

Yet as he scrounged through his small refrigerator and took out a couple of eggs to scramble, Nathan couldn't help wishing the woman with the beautiful green eyes could have found it in her heart to take a chance on him.

Chapter Seven

Sitting in the breezeway late on Friday afternoon, Catherine leaned back in the chaise longue and drew a weary breath. The week had been a disaster.

Nathan had not been as easy to replace as she'd expected.

When she'd called Becky last Sunday afternoon looking for recommendations, the real estate agent had warned her the itinerant handyman types on the island weren't always reliable. Nor could she vouch for their work. Each season brought a new, untested batch.

After passing along the few names she had, Becky had wished her luck.

In short order, Catherine had discovered she needed it. She'd ruled out the first three guys she interviewed less than five minutes after they'd arrived. The one with bloodshot eyes hadn't been able to put a complete sentence together. The second had seemed to know less about carpentry than she did. Candidate number three had spoken almost no English, and she'd spotted him swigging out of a beer bottle before he rang her bell—at eight in the morning.

So when Dennis Molini had shown up to be interviewed on Wednesday—clean, sober and seeming to possess *some* construction knowledge—she'd hired him. He'd started yesterday morning.

By earlier this afternoon, less than two days into the job, Catherine had known he wasn't going to work out.

First, he was sloppy. He left tools lying around to be tripped over, he'd gouged the wall while ripping out the musty carpet and his drywall-patching skills were pathetic.

Second, he was slow. Nathan had finished the first room in five days, except for the floor. And he'd done a beautiful job. In two days, the only thing Dennis had managed to do was rip out the carpet and repair a section of baseboard. Badly.

Third, he took long lunches and frequent breaks, which he spent smoking in the breezeway. Since he charged by the hour, the meter was adding up quickly.

Fourth, the loud music he'd played had driven her

crazy. She'd asked him to turn it down twice, but she hadn't noticed any appreciable decline in volume.

Finally, Zach hadn't liked him. Not that she blamed him, considering one of Dennis's ground rules to her had been, "Keep the kid out of my way." In hindsight, she should have known that was a bad sign. But she'd been desperate.

Not desperate enough to keep him on, however.

So ten minutes ago, after settling Zach in the living room with a video, she'd handed Dennis a check and said thanks but no thanks.

Meaning she was once again without any help.

And with only six weeks left to complete the renovations and finish the decorating, she was beginning to panic.

"Is he gone, Mom?"

At Zach's question, she looked toward the screen door that led into the kitchen. He was hovering inside, scoping out the breezeway to make sure the coast was clear.

"Yes, honey. And he won't be coming back."

Zach pushed through the door, relief etched on his features as he climbed into her lap. He'd been doing a lot of that since the spaghetti sauce incident, reverting to a degree of clinginess she hadn't seen in months.

"I'm glad. He wasn't very nice."

"No, he wasn't. And he didn't do very good work, either."

Tucking his head into her shoulder, Zach yawned. "Nathan did the bestest work. I miss him, Mom."

So did she. But admitting it wasn't going to help either of them. "I know, honey."

"Maybe he could come back and help us again."

"I'm sure he's working for someone else by now. I think I'll try to see what I can do myself. My toes are feeling a lot better."

He lifted his head and gave her a skeptical look. "Then how come you're still limping?"

There was nothing wrong with her son's observation skills.

"I'm just being careful."

He nestled against her again. She ought to get up and fix dinner. But she was exhausted. And so was Zach. The nightmares that had plagued him for the first few months after the shooting had come back with a vengeance. Several times each night his cries would send her hurrying to his room, where she'd remain until he quieted and fell back asleep. For the past two nights, she'd disregarded the psychologist's advice and let him sleep with her. The nightmares hadn't gone away, but they'd been less severe.

The spaghetti incident was the culprit, of course.

But she knew it had been compounded by the strong attachment he'd formed to Nathan in the week the two of them had spent together. An attachment that had been severed as swiftly as the one he'd had with his father.

Catherine's stomach growled, reminding her again it was dinnertime. But she didn't have the energy to get up and cook a meal just yet. For now, she was content to hold her son safe in her arms and relish the pressure of his soft, trusting body cuddled against her.

Sleep tugged at her eyelids, and she let them drift closed, trying to put aside worries about her renovation project and her son.

Not to mention the nagging feeling she'd made a big mistake letting Nathan go.

As Catherine led her son down the aisle of the small church she'd scouted out in a quick drive around the island yesterday, Zach suddenly tugged on her hand.

"Mom, look! Nathan's here!"

She jerked to a stop at his excited comment and followed the direction of his pointed finger. He was right. Even though she had only a back view, she recognized the chestnut hue of Nathan's hair, his broad shoulders and his steadfast posture.

It figured. Of all the churches on Nantucket,

she'd managed to choose the one Nathan attended. Not that there were dozens of options. But still…the coincidence was odd.

Zach gave her hand another urgent tug. "Can we go talk to him, Mom?"

She guided him into the closest pew and put her finger to her lips, motivated more by embarrassment than reverence. "The service is about to start, honey. And we have to be quiet in God's house."

He lowered his voice. "Can we talk to him afterward, then?"

The eager brightness that had been missing from her son's countenance for the past week had returned. She didn't have the heart to turn him down flat.

"We'll see."

Although the service was okay—she approved of the quiet piano music over a booming organ, and the minister seemed warm and personable— she couldn't concentrate. But the final few words of the sermon did snag her attention.

"Sometimes providence steps in where we fear to tread," the minister said. "The Lord has interesting ways of helping us focus on the things we know we need to do, but have put off out of fear or apathy. If we listen, He'll tell us when to move forward. When to hold back. When to let go. All we have to do is open our hearts to the signs all around us."

Catherine frowned. She'd never been a great believer in signs. And if the Lord had been telling her anything over these past two years, His message had fallen on deaf ears. She hadn't tuned Him in since the day David died.

Her thoughts traveled back to that fateful Sunday morning. She'd been sitting at the kitchen table, sipping a cup of coffee as she'd waited for David and Zach to return from their newspaper-and-cinnamon-roll run, when she'd heard the sirens. As was her custom at the time, she'd said a silent prayer for whoever was in need.

Never knowing it was David.

Never knowing the man she loved was bleeding to death on a cold tile floor a block away.

She'd said more prayers after the call came in from the police, alerting her that her husband was being transported to the hospital and that an officer would meet her there with her traumatized son. As she'd sped through the quiet streets, she'd begged the Lord to spare David's life. Pleaded with Him.

But when the chaplain met her in the E.R., she'd known at once that the Almighty had turned a deaf ear to her entreaties.

She hadn't talked to Him since.

The notion of signs niggled at her, though. It did seem odd that she'd pick the same church Nathan attended, that their paths would cross again when she was most in need of help with the house—and with Zach.

A quick glance confirmed that his presence was already having a positive impact on her son. Zach was fairly glowing as his worshipful gaze rested on the man who called him "champ." As for the house—her aching toes were still protesting the work she'd tried to do yesterday.

It would be good to have him back, for practical reasons.

On a personal level, however, she was far less comfortable with the idea. Yet her son's welfare had to come first. If Nathan's presence forced her to confront some serious issues—so be it, she decided.

As the piano struck up the notes of the closing hymn, she took Zach's hand and leaned close to whisper. "Let's leave before the crowd so no one steps on my sore toes."

He gave her a crestfallen look. "Aren't we going to talk to Nathan?"

"Yes. We'll wait for him on the lawn in front."

A smile split his face. "Okay. I bet he'll be happy to see us."

Catherine wasn't as confident of that. Not after the send-off she'd given him.

But maybe—if she was lucky—he would find it in his heart to be generous.

* * *

Nathan saw Catherine the moment he stepped out of the church. She was standing off to one side, Zach's hand in hers, the golden light of morning bathing her skin in a warm glow as their gazes met. She appeared to be waiting.

For him?

"So are you going to stand us up the way you did last week with J.C. and Heather?"

At Marci's question, Nathan looked over his shoulder. She and Christopher had followed him down the aisle, with J.C. and Heather bringing up the rear. As they reached the door, Christopher dropped back to talk to J.C.

"I'm not planning to. But I need to talk to someone first for a minute."

"Yeah? Who? I didn't think you knew many people here yet."

He motioned toward the duo off to the side. "The woman I was working for."

Marci's eyes narrowed as she gave Catherine a cool perusal. "The one who fired you?"

"She had her reasons." Nathan knew J.C. had filled Marci in on the details. These days, there were few secrets among the siblings—even if certain ones from the past remained hidden.

"I know. But she could have given you a chance."

"Maybe she realizes that now." He didn't hold out a lot of hope she'd changed her mind, but then again, why else would she be waiting for him?

"Okay. We'll mingle for a few minutes. Let us know the verdict." She gave his arm an encouraging squeeze.

As Nathan crossed the lawn, Catherine's expression was difficult to decipher. But there was only one word to describe Zach's: *delighted*.

Tugging free of Catherine's hand, the youngster ran toward him. "Hey, Nathan!"

He dropped to one knee, smiling at the little boy's enthusiasm. "Hi, champ. I missed you."

"I missed you, too. It's been real lonesome at home since you left."

Catherine joined them, and Nathan rose. There were shadows under her eyes that hadn't been there a week ago, and her features were strained, giving her face an angular tautness. She was also limping worse than she had been when he'd left.

"Hello, Nathan." A slight quiver ran through her words.

"Hi. Were you at the service?"

"Yes. We always went at home. For Zach's sake. I meant to go here. But things…got in the way. This is the first time we've attended. It seems like a nice church."

"It is." Her choppy, slightly breathless small talk

suggested she didn't know how to broach the subject she wanted to discuss. So he threw out an opening. "How's the project coming?"

"It's not."

Bingo.

"Haven't you been able to find anyone to finish it up for you?"

"I hired one guy. It didn't work out."

"He smoked a lot and played loud music and wasn't friendly," Zach piped up. "He didn't do very good work, either."

Catherine's lips twisted into a mirthless smile. "That about sums it up. I let him go Friday."

"Mom tried to do some work herself yesterday, but she almost fell off the ladder," Zach added.

Nathan frowned. "You were climbing on a ladder? With broken toes?"

A soft flush suffused her cheeks. "I thought I might be able to do the work myself. But my toes didn't appreciate my efforts. And hiking boots weren't designed for ladders."

Silence fell between them, softened a bit by the muted conversation and laughter behind them.

Assuming Catherine was trying to think of a diplomatic way to ask him to come back, he saved her the trouble.

"I'd be happy to help out again if you're willing to have me back."

"That would be awesome!" Zach's eyes lit up.

"I thought you might have another job by now." Relief smoothed some of the tension from Catherine's face.

"I do. Several. But they're all smaller. I can work them in around yours if you don't mind stretching your project out an extra week or two. I can still have it done well before your deadline."

"That would be great. For everyone involved." She dipped her head slightly toward Zach. "A certain trauma, followed by the disappearance of a friend, has led to some setbacks."

Nathan got the message. "Maybe my helping out will take care of two birds with one stone."

"That's what I'm hoping."

"Why are you guys talking about birds?" Zach gave the adults a puzzled look.

"It's just an old expression, champ." Nathan grinned at him. "Are you going to be ready to paint next week?"

"Yeah!"

"How about if I come by tomorrow afternoon?" He checked with Catherine.

"That would be perfect." She took Zach's hand, and there was warmth—and apology—in her eyes. "Thank you."

He smiled. "It's my pleasure."

"See you tomorrow, Nathan!" Zach waved

over his shoulder as Catherine led him toward the street.

Nathan waved back, watching until a privet hedge hid them from view.

"That seemed cozy."

At the comment, Nathan redirected his attention to his sister, who was strolling toward him.

"She wants me to come back."

"And…?"

"I'm going to."

Marci looked toward the spot where Catherine and Zach had disappeared, her expression speculative. "Cute little boy."

"Yeah."

"Pretty mother, too."

A subtle inflection in his sister's tone raised Nathan's antennas. "It's a job, Marci. Nothing more."

"I didn't say it was." She glanced to her right and tipped her head. "Hmm. That's interesting."

Checking out her line of sight, Nathan noticed Edith standing in a small cluster of people a dozen yards away. Watching them. When she realized they'd spotted her, she grinned and flapped a hand in their direction.

"What's interesting?" Nathan didn't have a clue what Marci's last comment meant.

"Edith has that look."

"What look?"

"Her matchmaker mode look."

He'd heard all about Edith's penchant for match-making from his siblings. But they'd had a lot more contact with her than he had.

"She hardly knows me, Marci. I'm away from the cottage most days at jobs. In my free time, I schlep my painting supplies all over the island and work on new pieces. When I am at the cottage, I keep to myself. And I doubt she knows Catherine at all."

"That's never stopped her before. And trust me, she has an uncanny ability to match up people who seem incompatible. Look at me and Christopher. Or Heather and J.C. Talk about unlikely pairings. But things worked out great." Marci sent Edith another thoughtful glance. "My guess, dear brother, is that she's set her sights on you."

"I don't think so."

She shrugged. "Have it your way. So are we on for brunch?"

"Yes. I'll meet you at your car."

"Okay. I'll extricate Christopher from Gladys. She always corners him after services to get free medical advice, and he's too nice to brush her off."

As Marci set off with a purposeful stride, Nathan once more looked toward Edith. And the thumbs-up she directed his way confirmed his sister's assessment. She was back in matchmaker mode.

He knew his siblings had tried to discourage her efforts during their courting days. As had Kate MacDonald, according to Heather. But Nathan wasn't averse to a little assistance in that department. He'd been out of circulation way too long, and his dating skills were beyond rusty.

At the same time, he had a feeling the Lighthouse Lane matchmaker might be off base in his case. Given the trauma Catherine had endured, it seemed unlikely she could put it far enough behind her to give him a fair chance in the romance department.

But if Edith wanted to put her efforts into pairing them up, he wasn't going to discourage her. Because despite the odds, he intended to do everything he could to convince Catherine he was a man worth loving. And he'd take all the help he could get to accomplish that goal.

Chapter Eight

"I think we did real good today, don't you, Nathan?"

Tapping down the lid on the paint can, Nathan stifled a smile as he regarded his "helper." Zach was spattered with white paint from head to foot. Good thing Catherine had dug up a child-size baseball cap for him or she'd have one challenging shampoo job tonight.

"We sure did, champ." Standing, he propped his fists on his hips, noting in his peripheral vision how Zach imitated his stance. This whole hero-worship thing was new to him—and more than a little scary. It was way too easy to fall off pedestals.

Putting that unsettling thought aside, he surveyed the room, pleased with his progress. Considering he was shoehorning this project in around the other jobs he'd committed to during the week he'd been away, things had shaped up nicely in the past five days.

The walls and ceiling had been repaired, and he'd applied the undercoat. Next week he hoped to finish painting this room and deal with whatever Catherine wanted done in the two bathrooms. Then he could turn his attention to installing the floor in both rooms. He estimated that would take at least a week.

That part of the project unnerved him. Flooring was expensive, and he had little expertise in that area. But when she'd hired him, Catherine had mentioned she'd installed the same kind of flooring herself in the past and could walk him through it. He was counting on that.

"What do you say we clean up our brushes and call it a day?" Nathan smiled down at Zach.

"Okay." The boy trotted behind him as he led the way to the bathroom. Turning the water in the sink on full, he washed out his brush. Zach imitated him, working the bristles as best he could with his chubby little fingers.

"Good job. It's important to get all the paint out, or the brushes will get stiff. That makes it a lot harder to…"

"Zach!"

At Catherine's alarmed call, Nathan moved to the doorway. She scanned the empty space, her features tightening.

"Where's Zach?"

"Right here." Nathan moved aside so she could see him at the sink.

Zach waved and grinned at her, oblivious to the waves of tension rolling off her. "Hi, Mom. We're cleaning brushes."

As he went back to work, her shoulders sagged and she ran her fingers through her hair. "I tried calling from the kitchen door. When no one answered, I…I got worried."

From the hitch in her voice, she'd been a whole lot more than worried, Nathan concluded. But she'd been like this all week. On edge. Hovering. Checking on Zach every few minutes.

Yet she'd kept her distance from him. He and Zach had gone back to eating in the breezeway together when he was there at lunchtime, but Catherine always found an excuse not to join them.

It hurt, but he understood.

He also understood her desire to protect Zach. He'd noticed it the first time he'd seen them, at Marci's wedding. But it had been amplified since the spaghetti sauce incident. To the point where it was becoming smothering.

He wondered if she realized that.

"We couldn't hear you call with the water running, Catherine. I'm sorry."

"It's okay. As long as he's all right." She rubbed

her palms on her jeans and limped toward the bathroom. "I better try to clean him up a little before I let him in the house."

The sudden ring of his cell phone startled them both, and Catherine jerked as Nathan fished it from his pocket.

"Sorry. Excuse me for a minute."

With a nod, she continued toward the sink while Nathan withdrew the phone.

"We need to get some of that paint off your hands and face, Zach."

"I can do it, Mom." Frustration nipped at Zach's words.

Turning away from the debate he was sure would ensue, Nathan pushed the talk button and greeted his caller.

"Nathan, it's Monica Stevens from Blue Water Gallery. I have some good news. I sold the painting of the blond-haired boy about twenty minutes ago."

For a second, Nathan thought the fresh paint fumes in the room were addling his brain. "I'm sorry…what did you say?"

She chuckled. "The first sale is always special. Congratulations."

"You mean…someone actually bought it? At that price?"

"My buyer considered it a bargain."

"Wow."

He could hear the smile in her voice when she responded. "I told you I had good instincts for spotting talent. Watch for a check in the mail. Are you working on some other things?"

"Yes."

"Bring them in when they're finished. I think we can do well together."

"I'll do that. Thanks."

As Nathan severed the connection, he tried to breathe. He'd just sold a painting for more money than he'd ever possessed—legally—at one time.

It was amazing.

"Nathan?" At Catherine's uncertain tone, he turned toward the bathroom. Zach's face and hands had been scrubbed pink-clean, but she now sported a faint streak of diluted paint on her cheek. "Is everything okay?"

He couldn't stop the grin that took charge of his lips. "Everything is great."

"You look like the way I feel on Christmas." Zach tipped his head and scrunched up his face as he studied Nathan.

"That's because I feel like it's Christmas." No matter how hard he tried, he couldn't get his grin under control.

"Are you going to share the good news?" The whisper of a smile tugged at Catherine's lips.

The invitation was too hard to resist. Besides, this kind of joy was too potent to be held inside. "I just sold my first painting."

In the silence following his announcement, Catherine gave him a stunned look. "You paint?"

"You know he paints, Mom." Zach rolled his eyes. "He's been painting here all day."

"No, honey. I think he means he paints pictures." She arched an eyebrow at him, seeking confirmation.

"That's right. I've been sketching for years, but I just started painting. My neighbor put me in touch with the woman who handled her late husband's work at The Blue Water gallery, and I stopped by last weekend with the two I'd finished, not expecting much. Certainly nothing like this." He shook his head, still trying to grasp the news. "Maybe it was a fluke."

"What kind of pictures do you paint, Nathan?" Zach asked.

"The one someone bought today was a little blond boy on a beach. As a matter of fact, he reminded me of you."

"Honest?" Zach's chest puffed out.

"Yep." Nathan picked up a damp rag from the floor. "Well…I better finish cleaning up so I can head home."

"Are we gonna see you again at church Sunday, Nathan?" Zach asked, his expression hopeful.

"I'll be there."

"Come on, Zach. It's dinnertime." Catherine placed her hands on her son's shoulders, putting him between the two of them. The soft smile she gave him warmed a long-cold place in his heart. "Congratulations, Nathan. I'm happy for you."

She started toward the door, but some irrepressible impulse propelled him forward. "Wait."

As she hesitated, he closed the distance between them. "You have some paint on your cheek. Let me get it off for you."

Leaning closer, he gently wiped the white smudge from her smooth skin with the rag.

She didn't move a muscle. In fact, she hardly seemed to be breathing. And when he looked into her appealing green eyes, mere inches away, he, too, had difficulty convincing his lungs to cooperate.

Sandwiched between them, Zach squirmed. "Did you get it off, Nathan? 'Cause I'm hungry."

"Yeah." The word came out hoarse, and he cleared his throat as he backed off.

Catherine maintained eye contact for another moment. He could see the frantic pulse fluttering in the hollow of her throat, mirroring the erratic beat of his own heart.

As if jump-starting her lungs, she sucked in a sharp breath. "Come on, Zach. Good night,

Nathan." Without a backward glance, she led the youngster out of the room. A few seconds later, he heard the screen door to the kitchen open and close.

Now it was his turn to breathe.

And worry.

Last week she'd let him go because of his parallels to the man who'd killed her husband.

Maybe this week she'd let him go because she didn't appreciate him invading her personal space.

He shouldn't have touched her.

Yet he wasn't sorry he had. The spontaneous move had given him a chance to notice the barely-there dusting of freckles across her nose. To inhale the sweet scent of her skin. To marvel at the gold flecks in her expressive eyes.

His impulsive gesture had been worth the risk.

If he was lucky, she'd cut him some slack, attribute his rashness to the elation prompted by his news. Keep him on because she needed his help.

And maybe—if he was lucky—before this job was over she'd *want* him around as much as she needed him around.

A few days ago, he wouldn't have given much credence to that outcome, despite Edith's successful track record with unlikely pairings. But a few days ago, he would also have laughed if someone had told him a customer would pay that kind of money for one of his paintings.

Today's sale had convinced him that anything was possible.

Perhaps, God willing, even breaking through the barriers Catherine had erected between them.

She'd forgotten it was Father's Day.

No surprise there, given all the excitement in her life of late. But her memory lapse was a major misstep. Catherine knew it as soon as the minister launched into his sermon.

Most clerics talked about fathers on this day. They drew parallels between the Heavenly Father and worldly fathers. Hammered home the attributes of a good father. Encouraged fathers to take a more active role in their children's lives.

This man—Reverend Kaiser, according to the bulletin she'd picked up last week—followed that pattern. He had a slightly different take on the subject, focusing more on family life than fatherhood, but there were plenty of references to moms and dads and kids.

Fortunately, Zach was busy paging through the colorful child's Bible she always brought for him on Sunday. He didn't seem to be paying any attention to the words being spoken from the pulpit.

Good. He didn't need to be reminded of the loss of his father. Not after the traumatic incident ten days ago. At least things were improving, now that

Nathan was back. Zach's nightmares had begun to recede and his clinginess was dissipating.

She glanced toward the man who'd managed to create a niche for himself in their lives. He was seated a few rows ahead on the other side, wearing a navy-blue jacket over an open-necked white shirt with blue pinstripes. In the weeks he'd been on the island, he'd filled out a little, his physique going from gaunt to trim and toned. He looked really good.

A bevy of butterflies took flight in her stomach, and she yanked her gaze away.

Get a grip, Catherine! The man is your employee. Nothing more. You don't want him to be any more.

Her mind processed the message. Accepted it.

But her heart balked, thanks to that simple, impersonal touch on Friday that had kept her awake for much of the past two nights.

It was ridiculous.

She couldn't have feelings for Nathan. He was an ex-con. A man who'd engaged in street fights—with knives. And he had the scars to prove it. He'd wielded a gun in a robbery. Aimed it at innocent people. Might have pulled the trigger.

But he also treated her son with kindness—and infinite patience. He didn't hold grudges when people made mistakes—like firing him. He was a reliable, conscientious employee. He painted pictures of little boys with blond hair.

How did one reconcile such disparate pieces of the same person? It didn't seem possible for the angry youth Nathan had described to her to turn into a caring, principled man with a steady, strong faith.

Yet the proof of that transformation was sitting a few pews away.

Could Dale Nelson have undergone a similar metamorphosis?

As the name of her husband's killer echoed in her mind, the glimmer of a headache began to pulse in her temple, and she reached up to massage it.

That was not the kind of question she wanted to contemplate on Father's Day.

But there it was. And she had a sinking feeling it wasn't going to go away.

The more important question, though, was how was she going to deal with it?

Closing her eyes, Catherine tuned out the Father's Day sermon and did something she hadn't done in two years. She prayed.

I think I'm going to need some help here, Lord. I wouldn't ask if I had anyone else to turn to. That's the truth of it, as You know. But if You're willing to overlook my motivation for seeking You out, could You send a little guidance and strength my way?

Because I think I'm about to embark on an emotional roller-coaster ride. And I'd like to finish it in one piece.

He didn't want her to get away.

Shouldering through the congregants ambling out of the church after the service, Nathan did his best to be polite as he forged ahead. But talking to Catherine was his priority, and if he happened to elbow a few people a little too firmly, so be it.

He'd taken a quick peek at her during the Father's Day–themed sermon, wondering if she was having a rough time with it. Based on her closed eyes and the faint furrows on her brow, he'd assumed she was. He didn't know what he could do to mitigate the melancholy memories it must have dredged up, but he knew he had to try.

Mother and son had gone no more than ten feet across the lawn when he emerged from the church, and in a few long strides, he caught up with them. "Good morning."

At his greeting, they both turned toward him.

"Hi, Nathan." Zach grinned up at him. "We're going to Downyflake. Wanna come?"

"I'm sure he has other plans, Zach." Catherine shifted a few feet away from the surge of people exiting the church, keeping a firm grip on her son's hand as they moved out of the line of traffic.

Nathan followed her lead. "Thanks for the offer, Zach. But I'm going to lunch with my family today." At the youngster's crestfallen expression, he tousled his head. "I bet you'll enjoy those sugar doughnuts anyway, though. They're great."

"Yeah." Zach's face brightened.

Giving Catherine his full attention, Nathan scrutinized her. Up close, she looked a little pale and— *stricken* was the word that came to mind.

"You okay?"

At his quiet question, she gave a slow blink. "Yes. Of course."

"I thought the sermon might have been a little difficult for you."

Instead of responding, she released Zach's hand and dug through her purse. Retrieving a pair of sunglasses, she slipped them on, hiding her eyes. Then she gripped her purse in front of her. Like a shield.

As silence fell between them, Nathan noted Zach in his peripheral vision. The youngster was sizing up a little boy about his age in an adjacent cluster of people. Zach took a step toward the child. The other little boy did the same. It appeared to be a friendship in the making. Good. Zach needed a friend.

So did Catherine. As desperately as her son.

But she was fighting it every step of the way. With him, anyway.

When it became apparent she didn't intend to respond to his remark about the sermon, Nathan switched to a less personal topic. "If it's okay, I think I'll come by tomorrow morning instead of in the afternoon. The light at the painting job I'm doing in Cisco will be better later in the day."

Her posture eased a fraction. "That's fine. I have some errands to run tomorrow, and I'd rather do them after lunch, anyway."

"Is the flooring still scheduled to arrive tomorrow?"

"Yes. Do you think you'll be ready for it by next week?"

"If all goes as planned. You mentioned when you hired me that you'd worked with it before?"

"Yes. I'm pretty handy when I don't have broken toes." The flicker of a smile flirted with her lips. "I did a lot of the remodeling work in our house in Atlanta."

"I'll welcome any advice you can give. I haven't dealt with that particular kind of flooring before."

"No problem." She turned, and a fleeting touch of panic crossed her face when she realized Zach wasn't beside her.

"He's over there." Nathan gestured a few feet away, where the two boys were engaged in an animated conversation.

"Zach!"

At her summons, he spoke to the other boy, then trotted over. "That's Adam, Mom. He goes to Sunday school here. Can I go next week, too?"

"We'll see."

"That means no." He folded his arms across his chest and stuck out his chin. "I'm never going to make any friends."

Nathan wasn't certain it was wise to jump into the mother/son exchange, but Zach did need friends his own age—and he wasn't certain Catherine recognized that. So he took the plunge. "Sure you will, champ. Your mom will find some ways for you to meet other kids. She knows that's important."

A slight frown appeared on Catherine's brow. He couldn't tell if it was prompted by disapproval or insight.

"Come on, Zach." She took her son's hand. "Let's head to Downyflake. See you tomorrow, Nathan."

He watched as they walked away. And hoped he hadn't just shot himself in the foot.

"We should be taking *you* out to celebrate at some swanky place, not the other way around," J.C. grumbled as Nathan led the way through the arbor entrance to The Chanticleer in 'Sconset.

"You guys have been treating me ever since I've

been here. And I have the money now." Nathan shot J.C. a grin over his shoulder.

"You didn't have to pick a pricey place like this. We'd have been happy with Arno's."

Heather jabbed her husband in the side with her elbow and smiled at Nathan. "I, for one, am grateful. I love this restaurant and don't get here often enough." She sent J.C. a pointed look before continuing. "And the garden is divine."

"It can't compare to the one at The Devon Rose, though." Marci gave the grounds a discerning sweep.

"Which is in a sad state of neglect this summer. Thanks to Junior." Heather laid her hand on her rounded tummy and sighed.

"Yeah. I think I did see a renegade weed or two the last time I was there. How dare they?" Marci grinned at her. "I'll tell you what. I'll come by and whip it into shape for you next week."

"You're busy enough with Caring Connections," Christopher protested, bringing up the rear as they trooped through the garden. "With the way it's taken off over the past year, the senior citizens on the island see you more than I do."

"You had me all to yourself for more than two weeks on our honeymoon."

"Yeah." A smile lifted the corners of his lips as he draped an arm around her shoulders. "That's true."

"So you won't miss me too much if I take a couple of hours to weed Heather's garden. You can thank Henry for my obsession with flowers, you know."

"Trust me, I know. Have you had a chance to get acquainted with him yet, Nathan?" Christopher asked.

"Yes. He invited me over for a visit when I met him at your wedding. I was treated to his banana-nut bread last week. And quite a few good stories." The older man was just as Marci had described him in her letters: affable, lively and enthusiastic. Ever since she'd told him how restoring Henry's garden had led to the romance that blossomed between her and Christopher, he'd looked forward to meeting the octogenarian.

"Henry's quite the storyteller," Christopher concurred as they took their seats at the open-air table Nathan had reserved, protected from the sun by a vine-covered overhang attached to the indoor part of the restaurant.

"I heard a few about the two of you, too." Nathan picked up a menu and began to peruse it.

"Yeah?" Marci narrowed her eyes. "Like what?"

"My lips are sealed."

"Fine." She took a quick glance at the menu, set it aside and refocused on her brother. "If you don't want to talk about Henry, tell us what's new with

Catherine. I spotted you talking to her again today after the service."

Nathan hoped the flush creeping up his neck stayed below his collar. "We didn't talk about anything worth repeating. Unless flooring interests you."

"Edith had her eye on the two of you again."

The flush crept higher.

"What's this about Edith? Have I been missing something?" J.C. looked from Marci to Nathan.

"No."

"Yes."

The two siblings spoke simultaneously. Marci smirked. Nathan frowned.

"The Lighthouse Lane matchmaker has her sights set on Nathan." Marci gave Nathan a smug look.

"Then she's going to be disappointed," Nathan countered.

Marci ignored that comment. "So tell us something about Catherine we don't know."

"Okay." Nathan decided to drop her a crumb. "She played the violin at your wedding."

His sister's eyes widened. "You're kidding."

"Nope."

"You met her at my wedding?"

"No. We just saw each other."

"As in 'Some Enchanted Evening'? Across a crowded room and all that? How romantic!"

"It was daylight and we were outside."

Marci shrugged. "Same difference. Did she…"

"The flounder sounds good to me," Christopher interrupted. "What are you going to have, Nathan?"

"The scallops." He sent his brother-in-law a grateful look.

"I'm going with the Vermont brie and wild mushroom omelet." Heather closed her menu.

"What are you having, Marci?" Christopher asked.

"I don't know. I haven't had a chance to read the menu."

"That's because you've been too busy grilling your brother. Leave the poor guy alone. He's paying the bill, after all." Christopher grinned at Nathan. "Can I order dessert, too, if I get my wife off your back?"

"Cute, Christopher." Marci made a face at him before pinning Nathan with a warning look. "Okay, fine. I'll let you eat in peace. But I'm only deferring this discussion to another day."

Heather chuckled. "These Clay kids are tough."

Grinning, J.C. put his arm around her. "You want me to change?"

She snuggled closer to him. "No way."

Christopher followed J.C.'s example and tugged Marci close. "Heather's right. You guys are tough.

But I wouldn't want you any other way, either." He brushed his lips across her temple.

As Nathan watched the exchanges, it was clear his brother and sister had made good matches. There was contentedness about them, a rightness in the pairings, that left him with a warm feeling—and more than a little envy.

He'd like to find that kind of love someday. With someone like Catherine—or perhaps Catherine herself.

But while there had been obstacles to his siblings' matches, they were minor compared to the one between him and the woman who played the violin with such heart-rending emotion.

And hard as he tried to remain optimistic, to cling to the hope that had buoyed him up the day he'd sold his painting, he was fast losing confidence he would find a way to overcome it.

Chapter Nine

❧

She felt like a spy.

Torn, Catherine shifted her purse on her shoulder and regarded the door to the Blue Water Gallery. Ever since Nathan had told her three days ago that he was a painter—in the artistic sense—she'd been intrigued. As long as she was in town, why not satisfy her curiosity? The gallery was a public place, after all. Anyone could walk in off the street and look at the offerings.

Yet she couldn't shake the feeling she was somehow invading his privacy.

"Why are we stopping here, Mom?" Yawning, Zach dug into the cup of mint chocolate-chip ice cream she'd treated him to at The Juice Bar. After traipsing around after Nathan all morning, he was ready for a nap.

"I have to check on something real quick. Then we'll head home, okay?"

"Okay."

Hoping the ice cream would keep him occupied for a few minutes, she stifled her guilty feelings and stepped inside the gallery. A wooden, backless bench hugged one of the walls in the foyer, and she guided him to it. Perfect. No way would the owner want a sticky-fingered child wandering around. Plus, from this spot, she could keep an eye on him while she made a quick circuit of the rooms that opened off the entry area. If she was lucky, Nathan's second painting would be in one of them.

"Wait here, Zach. I'll be right back. I'm just going to look in these two rooms. You can see me the whole time, okay?"

"Can I come?" He gave the gallery an interested perusal.

"Only if you throw away your ice cream. There's no food allowed."

She waited while he debated this choices. As she'd expected, the ice cream won.

"I'll stay here."

That problem solved, she started her circuit of the first room, scrutinizing the paintings for signatures.

Less than sixty seconds later, a tall woman emerged from the back of the gallery. She gave Zach a quick glance before continuing toward Catherine.

"Don't worry. He has strict instructions to stay on the bench," Catherine assured her. She'd expected someone to appear, and she had her story ready.

The woman smiled. "I wasn't concerned. He appears to be a well-behaved young gentleman. I'm Monica Stevens, the owner. May I assist you with anything?"

"I'm just browsing. Your place looked interesting, and I thought I'd stop in for a quick peek."

"Take your time. If you have any questions, let me know. I'll be in the room at the end of the foyer hall."

After confirming that Zach was still intent on his ice cream, Catherine waited until the woman retraced her steps, then resumed her search. She had no clue what she was looking for in terms of either style or subject matter. All she knew was that Nathan's first painting had featured a blond-haired little boy. But in her initial scan of the room she hadn't spotted any paintings of children.

She had almost completed her circle of the first room when she found it.

And it was nothing like she'd expected.

At first glance, she thought it was a landscape. A long strip of sand stretched toward the horizon, and though the foreground was lit by the sun, the distant clouds that were massed in the background and the whitecaps on the sea warned of a coming squall. There was a stunning power to the scene, and a slight impressionistic feel added to its evocativeness.

She was impressed.

But she was even more impressed when she drew close and discovered it wasn't a landscape at all. It was a portrait—of a very different kind. There was only one figure in the scene, and it was small. But it was the focal point of the painting, and it vaulted the piece from very good to extraordinary.

Moving in, Catherine studied the dark-haired little boy in the distance. Still in the sunshine, his back to the clouds, he was oblivious to the approaching storm. Toting a bucket of water from the sea to a moat he'd dug around a sandcastle, he was the picture of innocence—unaware that his quest to fill the hole was futile and his efforts to protect his castle were hopeless. For soon the shadows would overtake him. The storm would come. His stronghold would be demolished.

The scale of the child in the painting was masterful, Catherine realized. By placing him in a vast landscape, Nathan had clearly communicated that he was not only oblivious to the approaching tempest, but vulnerable to forces beyond his control.

The scene conveyed a hushed, ominous sense of impending danger, of innocence lost, that sent a shiver snaking down her spine.

"It's remarkable, isn't it?"

Startled by the question, Catherine turned to find that the gallery owner had returned. She had no idea how long she'd been rooted to the spot, mesmerized by Nathan's painting, but a quick peek confirmed that Zach was still occupied with his ice cream.

"Yes, it is."

The woman stepped beside Catherine and examined the canvas. "There's a lot more to that piece than meets the eye."

"I agree." But she didn't want to discuss Nathan's painting. The owner might mention to him that someone had expressed an interest in it—and she didn't want him to know she'd stopped in. Because now that she'd seen his work, felt its power, sensed it came from deep within his soul, her visit *did* seem like an invasion of privacy. "Well, thank you for letting me look around. I'll try to stop in again some day when I have more time."

"You're always welcome."

Returning to the foyer, Catherine snagged Zach's hand and led him out the door, into the sunlight. She spotted a trash container nearby, and disposed of the empty cardboard cup.

"What was that place, Mom?" Zach trotted along beside her as they headed up India Street toward their car.

"People who have things to sell bring them there, and that lady you saw tries to find other people to buy them." Vague but true, she rationalized.

"How come you didn't buy anything?"

"I didn't see anything I wanted."

That was true, too, Catherine reflected, as they crossed the street, Zach's hand firmly tucked in hers. For while she'd admired Nathan's painting, its menacing undertones had disturbed her. As the gallery owner had suggested, there were layers to his piece. It wasn't just about an approaching storm. It was about looming, unseen threats. And endangered innocence.

But what did it all mean in relation to Nathan?

That question burned in Catherine's mind—and in her heart—as they headed out of town on Surfside Road. Somehow, she sensed this painting held the key to Nathan's past. And she wanted to know more.

But she doubted her curiosity would ever be satisfied. Because no way did she intend to tell him she'd visited the gallery. It would suggest she was interested in him beyond their employer-employee relationship. And she wasn't.

Was she?

As that disturbing question echoed in her mind, a horn blared to her right, and she jammed on her brakes. Too late. She was already halfway across the intersection. Accelerating, she got out of the way. Fast. And hoped there weren't any cops nearby.

"Hey, Mom, weren't you supposed to stop at the corner?" Zach twisted around to look back at the crossroads.

"Yes, honey. I should have been paying more attention."

"Nathan says you should always pay attention when you're doing something important, or you can make mistakes. Maybe even get hurt."

The man was right. Those were the exact things she wanted to avoid in her car.

And with him.

"That's true, honey. I'll be more careful next time."

About everything, she resolved. And that meant avoiding any situation that could put a more personal slant on her relationship with the man she'd hired.

Like visits to art galleries.

Three days later, as Nathan was reattaching a loose baseboard in one of the guest bathrooms at what would soon be Sheltering Shores Inn, a woman's scream pierced the air.

Catherine's.

Dropping his hammer, he vaulted to his feet and took off running.

He met her in the breezeway as she stumbled out the screen door, her eyes awash with terror.

"Catherine, what is it?"

She pushed past him, heading for the door that led into the backyard. "Zach's hurt. Oh, God, please! I can't lose him, too!" The anguished cry was torn right from her heart.

He was on her heels as she choked out the words, and once past the door, a quick survey of the yard told him she wasn't overreacting. Zach lay on his back on the ground beside the split-rail fence, an overturned bucket beside him.

And he wasn't moving.

Leaving Catherine behind, Nathan sprinted toward the child, doing his best to rein in his own panic.

But it was a losing battle.

Partly because he hated to see any child hurt.

And partly because he was the one who'd sent Zach out to the backyard—unsupervised—to empty a bucket of dirty water he hadn't wanted to pour down the newly cleaned porcelain in the bathrooms. If anything happened to her son, Catherine would never forgive him.

Nathan got to Zach first and went down on one

knee beside him. The little boy stared up at him, wide-eyed, struggling to breathe.

The immediate problem was easy for Nathan to diagnose. Zach had had the wind knocked out of him. You got to know a lot about that kind of stuff from street fights.

He hoped that was all that was wrong.

Catherine dropped to the ground beside him. He could feel her shaking as she reached out to her son. "Zach, honey, lay still, okay?"

At her shaky words, Zach looked at her. The alarm in his eyes ratcheted up another notch.

Her panic was exacerbating the situation.

"Catherine, let me deal with this." Without waiting for her assent, Nathan took Zach's hand, refocusing the little boy's attention on him. "Hey, Zach. You're fine. You just knocked all the wind out of your lungs when you fell, and they're surprised. But they'll start working again in a minute." He strove for a calm, soothing tone and forced his stiff lips to curve into a smile.

"I…can't…"

Nathan pressed a gentle finger to Zach's lips as the little boy tried to gasp out a few words. "Don't talk for a minute, okay? Let your lungs concentrate on breathing instead of making words. I bet you feel like a whole bunch of bricks are sitting on your chest, don't you?"

The youngster gave a nod and clung to his hand, his fingers small and trusting. Nathan swallowed past the lump that rose in this throat. "I bet you decided to climb up on that fence to check out how far you could see, didn't you?"

Another nod.

"I did that once. I slipped and fell on my back, too. I couldn't breathe, either, at first. It was real scary." Nathan didn't tell him it was a tall chain-link fence. Or that he was an adult up to no good. Or that the cops were closing in on him. "You know, I was thinking that before I come out tomorrow to finish up in the bathroom, maybe I'll swing by Downyflake and pick up a few dough-nuts. Would you like that?"

"Yeah."

The youngster's respiration was beginning to even out, Nathan noted, watching the rise and fall of his chest.

"Okay. Sugar?"

"Yeah. They're the best."

"You got it, champ." He smiled and stroked the little boy's hand. "You breathing better now?"

"Yeah."

"Good. Does anything hurt? Your arms or your legs?"

Zach wiggled the extremities in question. "Nope."

"Then you can get up. But slow, okay? Until we make sure everything else checks out."

Slow wasn't in Zach's vocabulary, as Nathan had learned early on, so he kept a firm grip on him as the boy stood. Then he gave him a swift but thorough appraisal. His color was good, he didn't appear to be in any pain and his eyes were clear and focused.

Crisis averted.

The tension in Nathan's shoulders eased.

Until Zach suddenly frowned. "Hey, Mom, are you sick?"

As Nathan shifted toward Catherine, his tension returned in a flash.

She was sitting on the ground beside him, her whole body quivering. All the color had drained from her face, and a thin film of sweat had beaded on her upper lip. Her respiration was shallow, her eyes glassy. She looked like she was in shock.

The crisis with Zach might be over, but it was clear he now had another one on his hands.

Gripping her upper arms, he spoke in the same calm, gentle tone he'd used with Zach. "Catherine, it's okay. Zach's not hurt. Take a few deep breaths. Catherine?"

When he exerted a bit of pressure on her arms, she blinked and transferred her attention to him.

He tried for a smile as he put one arm around Zach and drew the boy close beside him. "Zach's right here, Catherine. He's fine. Come on, sweet-heart, take a few deep breaths for me, okay?"

She blinked again. Drew one shuddering breath. Another. Some of the glassiness in her eyes dissipated.

"Good girl."

"Is she sick, Nathan?"

At Zach's worried question, Nathan hugged him. "No, champ. She was just worried about you. When you love someone a lot, you get scared if you think they might be hurt. Your mom loves you a whole bunch, so she got really scared when you fell."

"But I'm okay." He leaned over and touched Catherine's cheek. "I'm not hurt, Mom. You don't have to be scared."

She grasped his hand. Closed her eyes as she pressed it against her cheek. Sucked in a lungful of air. Then pulled him into a fierce, tight embrace.

"Hey, Mom, you're squeezing me to death!" Zach protested, squirming to free himself.

In the end, Nathan had to gently pry her hands off her son. "You need to let him go, Catherine, so he can breathe," he said softly.

When she at last relinquished her grip, Nathan smiled at the little boy. "What do you say we all go inside? I bet you wouldn't mind having a cookie before you take your nap."

"I had one after lunch."

"I think I can talk your mom into letting you have another." He winked at the youngster.

"Yeah?" His expression grew hopeful. "That would be good."

"Okay. Let's head in." He stood, then took Catherine's hand and drew her to her feet. Tremors continued to course through her, and he slipped an arm around her shoulders as he turned toward the house. Instead of protesting, as he feared she might, she leaned against him. On his other side, Zach reached for his hand.

Flanked by a vulnerable, trusting little boy and a shattered woman who were both counting on him for support, an unfamiliar emotion tightened Nathan's throat. He'd never been anyone's anchor. Nor felt so needed. Or valued. Or worthy.

Warmth spilled from his heart, radiating throughout his body.

And in that instant, he knew that this moment was a sample of what he'd been yearning for his whole life. He wanted to be part of a circle of love. Not just in a traumatic time of need, but for always.

When they reached the breezeway, he gave Zach's fingers a squeeze. "Could you open the door for us?"

"Sure."

Releasing his hand, Zach pushed through and held it open.

Nathan scrutinized Catherine again as they eased through the door. She still hadn't spoken, nor had she stopped quivering. But a little color had seeped back into her cheeks.

"Why don't you sit here in the breezeway while I get a cookie for Zach and put him down for his nap. Okay?"

She gave a barely perceptible nod as he guided her to the wicker settee. Sinking down, she wrapped her arms around her body as if she was trying to hold herself together.

"I'll be right back," Nathan promised.

Again, she dipped her head.

"Come on, champ. Let's round up that cookie."

Nathan took care of the cookie business as fast as he could, setting it on a plate and pouring a half glass of milk. To Zach's delight, he suggested they take it upstairs so he could enjoy it in his room.

"Wow! Mom never lets me eat in bed. Except when I'm sick."

"We'll make an exception today." Nathan handed the plastic cup to Zach and led the way up to his bedroom. Once he'd settled the child in with the snack and a picture book, he hotfooted it back to the breezeway. Zach's trauma was over.

But he had a feeling Catherine's was still in full swing.

In the five minutes he'd spent with Zach, Catherine hadn't changed position. She was sitting as he'd left her, arms wrapped around her body, still trembling, still too pale. But the numbed shock in her eyes had given way to an almost palpable distress.

As he approached, he also caught the glimmer of tears. The woman who'd said she never cried looked as if her control was finally about to break.

Joining her on the settee, he entwined his fingers with hers. She clung to them, her grasp painfully tight.

"Thank you for t-taking care of Zach."

"He didn't need much taking care of. I'm more worried about his mom."

Her lips twitched as if she was trying to summon up a smile. Instead, they began to tremble. A tear slipped past her lower lashes and began to creep down her cheek. She didn't seem to notice…and he resisted the temptation to wipe it away, not wanting to call attention to it.

"Yeah. His mom's a mess, isn't she?"

"I wouldn't use that adjective."

"Why not? It's true." She blinked and shook her head. "I t-try so hard to keep him safe. That's why I moved here. My family v-visited Nantucket once, when I was a teenager, and I remembered it as a quiet, sheltered kind of place. I wanted Zach to g-grow up in that kind of environment so I wouldn't have to worry about him all the time. But I couldn't even keep him safe in our own yard. He could have b-broken his neck." The last word caught on a sob.

He stroked the back of her hand with his thumb. "Accidents happen everywhere, Catherine," he said gently. "It wasn't your fault."

"I feel like it was. I should have been watching him."

"You can't watch him every minute."

"But I'm so afraid of losing him, too! He's all I have now. If anything ever happened to him…" Her face crumpled, and she dropped it into her hands, trying to stifle the sobs clamoring for release.

"Oh, Catherine." His stomach contracted, and he touched the silky strands of hair that had fallen across her cheek. Tucked them behind her ear. Then he followed his instincts and wrapped her in his arms, pulling her against his chest. Close to his heart. "Let it out, sweetheart. You're overdue for a good cry."

"I—I don't cry." Her broken protest was muffled against his shirt, but she didn't try to pull away. Nor could she stop the sobs that began to wrack her slender body. They shuddered through her in waves; harsh, ragged sounds that disrupted the quiet Nantucket air and expressed more eloquently than words all the grief, anguish and anger that been building inside her for the past two years.

At some point, Nathan shifted enough to fish a handkerchief out of his pocket. She took it without a word and continued to cry.

He had no idea how long he held her in the shelter of his arms, but when at last her tears subsided, she eased back. Keeping her head bowed, she blew her nose.

"Sorry about that."

"Don't be. After all you've been through, you deserve a good cry."

"Tears don't solve problems."

"No. But they can help dispel strong emotion."

She lifted her tear-stained face. Even with blotchy skin and red-rimmed eyes, she looked beautiful to him. "You sound as if you're speaking from experience."

"I've shed my share of tears." Some long ago, in the darkness of the terrible nights. Others over the past two years, as he fought his way back from the black abyss that had become his life.

"Most men wouldn't admit that." She studied his face.

He lifted one shoulder. "That's their issue."

Dabbing at her eyes with his handkerchief, she

continued to watch him. "You're a different sort of person, Nathan Clay."

"Yeah." He tried to smile, but all he managed was a small quirk on one side of his mouth. "An ex-con."

"That's not what I meant."

"It's true, though." He was glad that hadn't been top of mind when she'd made her comment. But his background did set him apart. And it always would. If there was to be any future for the two of them, his history couldn't be swept into a dark corner. It had to be recognized and accepted.

"I was thinking more about your kindness and sensitivity and patience." She looked down, balling his handkerchief into her fist.

A little seed of hope sprouted to life in his heart. "Thank you."

"You're very good with Zach, too. A lot of guys would consider him a nuisance—like the short-lived remodeler I hired after you left. I like that about you. You've been a great blessing in his life. In both our lives." Her shoulders drooped. "I've tried my best to be all things to him these past two years, but it's hard going it alone."

She'd called him a blessing.

Incredible.

"You're not alone." His words rasped and he cleared his throat. "The man upstairs is always just a holler away. And I wield a mean hammer if you ever need anything repaired."

"I'm not on the best of terms with God. And as for repairs…" She sighed. "A hammer and nails can't fix loneliness. Or a broken heart."

Disregarding the red alert that began to flash in his mind, Nathan angled toward her. With a gentle finger, he lifted her chin until her gold-flecked eyes were looking into his. "I'm sorry for all your losses, Catherine. I can't fix those, but I can return some of the compliments you just paid me. In the weeks since we met, I've come to admire your ability to pick up the pieces of your life and move on. I've been impressed by your strength. And by your commitment to Zach. You're a different sort of person, too, Mrs. Walker."

"In spite of my meltdown today?"

"You had good reason for it."

His finger was still under her chin, and it seemed the most natural thing in the world to take the next step and cup her face with his hands. Her skin was smooth against his calloused palms, and as he stroked his thumbs over the faint shadows beneath her eyes, the sudden surge of longing in her green irises blindsided him.

Because it mirrored the yearning in his heart.

Kissing Catherine hadn't been on his agenda

for today. But all at once, it was the only thing that mattered.

No matter the risk.

Drawing in a steadying breath, he bent his head and tenderly pressed his lips to hers.

More than ten years had passed since he'd kissed a woman. Longer still since such an embrace had involved tenderness and caring. But as he claimed Catherine's sweet lips, he felt as if he'd been transported to a different realm. To a world where affection and warmth and gentleness ruled. Where devotion and commitment were more than words. Where honor and vows and love wove a beautiful tapestry.

And as her mouth stirred beneath his, responding to his touch, he knew this moment, fragile as a butterfly's wing, would live forever in his memory.

When he at last drew back, her face still cupped in his hands, she was trembling again.

So was he.

Brushing a wisp of hair away from her forehead, he took one of her hands in his. He didn't intend to ruin the moment by talking about it. Or apologizing. Or saying things she might not be ready to hear. It was better to leave now. Give them both a chance to regroup. To process what had just happened.

Clearing the huskiness from his throat, he gave

her hand a squeeze. "I need to head out. I've got another customer expecting me in twenty minutes. Will you be okay?"

"Yes." Her whispered response was barely there, her eyes big as she regarded him.

He stood. "Call me if you need anything."

She nodded.

"I'll see you tomorrow."

Another silent nod.

Lifting a hand in farewell, he pushed through the door, strode toward his bike and took off down the dirt road—all the while trying to assess Catherine's reaction to the kiss.

Surely she'd been as surprised by it as he'd been. Yet she hadn't pushed him away. Nor had she fired him again.

But where did they go from here? Would she think of his kiss as nothing more than a compassionate gesture? His way of comforting her after a nasty scare? Or would she see it for what it was— a desire to take their relationship to another level?

Nathan didn't know. But he hoped—and prayed—she would find a way to get past the parallels between him and the man who'd taken the life of her husband. To look into his heart and see the goodness he had to offer.

Yet luck had been elusive in his life. Although her acceptance of his kiss had been a positive sign, after a good night's sleep she might very well regret their little interlude and send him packing.

As if to verify that conclusion, rain began to fall from the clouds that had gathered during the past hour. Meaning long before he got back to town, he'd be hosed.

If he wasn't already.

Chapter Ten

This is ridiculous.

Bunching the sheet in her fists, Catherine expelled a frustrated breath and checked the clock atop her nightstand. Three-thirty. At this rate, she'd be lucky to get two hours of shut-eye tonight.

All because of a kiss that still lingered on her lips…and a whispered endearment.

No one had ever called her sweetheart.

Resigned to her sleepless state, she tossed the covers aside and swung her legs over the side of the bed. Maybe more housework would help tire her out. She'd been using her toes as an excuse to delay those kind of chores, but the swelling and bruising had faded. In another two weeks, she could ditch the hiking boots and go back to wearing regular shoes.

After pulling on jeans and a sweatshirt, she

headed downstairs, determined to take control of her thoughts—and emotions. Laundry first, she decided, veering toward the washer and dryer.

But her plan was foiled within two minutes. For as she sorted through the garments, her hands stilled on an article that had been missing from her clothes basket for two years.

A man's handkerchief.

Damp with tears.

Hers.

Catherine closed her eyes.

It was no use. Since their kiss twelve hours ago, she'd tried every trick in the book to put Nathan out of her mind. She'd scrubbed the bathrooms, pulled weeds from around the hydrangea bushes in front, cooked dinner, read Zach stories. Anything to keep from facing the disturbing questions and impulses generated by that brief moment of affection.

Had she been wise, she'd have pushed him away when he leaned toward her. She'd have refused to let herself be swayed by those appealing, warm brown eyes. But, no. She'd not only let him kiss her, she'd kissed him back.

She could try attributing that lapse in judgment to her distress over Zach and her heightened emotions after his fall.

Except that was a lie.

She'd let Nathan kiss her for one simple reason.

She'd wanted to be kissed.

And she'd liked it.

Just as she'd liked it when he'd called her sweetheart.

Tossing his handkerchief into the washer, she spotted the Atlanta Braves jersey he'd worn the day of the spaghetti incident. It had been sitting in her laundry room ever since.

Somehow it had never made it into the wash.

Slowly she leaned over and picked it up. Lifted the fabric close to her face. Inhaled the scent that was equal parts honest physical labor and powerful masculinity.

The scent that was all Nathan.

She should know, after getting an up close and personal whiff of it just twelve hours ago.

And Lord help her, she wanted more.

Setting aside the jersey, she closed the lid on the washer and twisted the dial. Then she wandered into the kitchen, made herself a cup of tea, sat at the kitchen table…and faced the truth.

She was falling for a man who represented everything she hated.

Or did he?

For despite the labels society might put on Nathan—troublemaker, delinquent, armed robber, ex-con—he didn't fit her criminal stereotype. Nathan Clay was living proof people could change.

Whatever his past, he'd become a compassionate, caring man who'd treated her and Zach with nothing but kindness and empathy and consideration.

That was the reason she'd kissed him back. Not because she was distraught or lonely or needed comforting. But because she was attracted to him—for all the right reasons.

And that was the crux of her problem. If she accepted that Nathan was a man worth loving; that he'd effected a radical transformation in his life; that his past was less important than his present—how did she know the same wasn't true for Dale Nelson?

Yet could she let go of her hate? Could she forgive the man who had destroyed her world if he, too, had changed and come to regret what he'd done? And what if he hadn't? Absent his remorse, could she still dredge up forgiveness, find it in her heart to ask the Lord to show him mercy?

All these months, she'd held on to her hate, using it to keep sorrow at bay. She'd been afraid to face her grief, fearing that if she gave into it, it would consume her and leave her spent and empty and shattered. But yesterday, in Nathan's arms, she'd let a lot of it go. And she felt okay. Better, even. Precisely *because* Nathan's strong, comforting arms had been ready to catch her if she started to fall toward the yawning abyss of inconsolable sorrow.

As for Dale Nelson…she needed to think that through. Pray about it, perhaps. For just as Nathan had found his future only by letting go of his unhappy past, she had a feeling the same was true for her.

But there was another piece of her past she had to leave behind, as well, she realized with a pang. A happy part.

It was time to say goodbye to David, too. To let him go. To know that while every memory they'd shared, every moment of their years together, would always be precious to her, it was okay to love someone else. To let another man claim a piece of her heart in his own special, unique way that would take nothing away from the love that had belonged only to her and David.

Rising, Catherine tossed her spent tea bag in the trash.

For the past two years, she'd been living in the past, focused on making it through each new day.

Maybe now it was time to think about the future.

"Mom! I can do it myself!"

At Zach's frustrated protest, Nathan looked toward the little boy. Catherine had been hovering over her son all day, never letting him more than a few feet from her sight, stepping in whenever he needed help, constantly warning him to be careful.

Yesterday's scare had obviously unnerved her.

He knew her actions reflected her deep love for her son, but her excessive attention was only annoying Zach.

She'd even cut his sandwich into bite-size pieces at lunch, much to Zach's disgust.

"He does a good job collecting all the tools, Catherine. And I don't leave any of the dangerous ones lying around." Nathan kept his tone mild, purging any hint of criticism. He'd been treading carefully since he'd arrived this morning. While she hadn't mentioned their kiss, she'd been avoiding eye contact. Not a good sign.

She shot him a quick glance. "The hammer's heavy. He might drop it on his foot."

"Oh, Mom!" Zach huffed out a breath. "Just because you dropped a paint can on your toes doesn't mean I'm going to drop a hammer. Besides, it's not heavy enough to break anything. And *I* have shoes on."

A flush crept up her neck as the phone in the main house began to ring.

"I'll keep an eye on Zach if you want to get that," Nathan offered.

She hesitated a second, then turned on her heel and exited.

"Sheesh." Zach gave Nathan a put-upon look and rolled his eyes. "Mom's all over me today. Worse than usual."

Nathan snapped the toolbox closed and brushed off his hands, taking a quick survey of the room, now finished except for the flooring. "That's because she loves you, champ. She got scared yesterday when you fell."

"Yeah." Zach stood and brushed his hands off, too. "She gets scared a lot. I bet she wouldn't be so nervous if my dad was still here." He sighed and scuffed the toe of his sport shoe on the subfloor. "I wish I had a dad again."

"Maybe you will, someday."

"Yeah?" Zach gave him a hopeful look. "How would I get one?"

"Well, if your mom found someone else to love, like she loved your dad, maybe she'd marry him. Then you'd have a new dad."

Narrowing his eyes, Zach sized him up. "Are you married, Nathan?"

Uh-oh. He should have seen that coming.

"No. And I'm too busy to think about that right now." He flipped off the light in the bathroom, dropped a hand to the boy's shoulder and tried to change the subject. "Next week we're going to start on the floor. After that, your mom can decorate the rooms. I bet your guests are going to like this place, don't you?"

"Yeah. So are you going to think about getting married *someday*?"

His evasive maneuvers hadn't worked. No surprise there. Zach could be as tenacious as a Nantucket deer tick when he bit into a subject that interested him. "I might. But you have to fall in love with someone first."

"You like my mom, don't you?'

This was getting really sticky. "Sure. She's a nice lady. I like her son, too." He forced his lips into a grin, trying to come up with some way to distract the youngster. "I think we should have a wrap party after this job is finished, don't you?"

"What's that?"

The mention of a party had done the trick. Good. "It's a celebration you have when a project is finished. We could have cake and ice cream, maybe."

Zach's eyes brightened. "Like a birthday?"

"Sort of."

"I like cake. And ice cream, too. I bet we could talk Mom into it."

"Zach!" Catherine's voice interrupted their conversation. "Naptime."

His face fell. "I hate naps."

Smiling, Nathan gave him a gentle push toward the door. "You'll outgrow them soon. Go on, your mom's waiting. We don't want her to worry. And this will give you a chance to ask her about that party."

"Yeah." Zach picked up his pace, clearly a man on a mission. "See you later, Nathan."

"See you, champ."

Once the little boy disappeared through the door, Nathan finished the cleanup. Ten minutes later, as he was placing the last folded tarp on top of the pile, Catherine joined him, surveying the room from the doorway.

"This turned out great, Nathan."

"Thanks." He wiped his hands on a rag, watching her. He'd been afraid Zach would mention their conversation about marriage, but if he was lucky, the boy's total focus had been on the proposed celebration.

Her next comment confirmed that, for once, Lady Luck has smiled on him.

"Zach said you mentioned a party to celebrate when the project is finished. He seems to think it includes singing, along with ice cream and cake."

Chuckling, he tossed the rag on top of the pile of tarps. "I called it a *wrap* party—with a w. No singing involved."

A smile tugged at her lips. "I like the idea. And Zach loves parties."

She was keeping her distance, hovering at the door rather than stepping into the room. As off balance as he was by the kiss they'd shared yesterday, judging by her behavior.

He considered bringing it up. But he was still grappling with his own feelings. For now, it might be better to table that discussion.

There was another issue he *did* want to bring up to her, however. One just as sensitive and potentially explosive. If he hadn't come to care so much for Zach, he might leave it alone. But Catherine's smothering attention, though prompted by love, was doing more harm than good. He hoped a few diplomatic hints might help her see the light.

It was worth the risk. For Zach's sake.

Propping a shoulder against the newly painted wall, he shoved his hands into the pockets of his jeans. "Did you get him down okay for his nap?"

"Amid much protest. The nap will be history, anyway, come September when he goes to kindergarten." A subtle tightening gave her features a fragile brittleness. "That's going to be a difficult transition."

"For him or for you?"

At his gentle question, she shrugged. "Both, maybe."

"Zach seems ready to make some friends. Eager, even."

She folded her arms across her chest. Not a good sign. "Letting him head out alone into the world worries me."

"I doubt the kindergarten class on Nantucket is a dangerous place." He let the hint of a smile play at his mouth, trying to coax her to relax a little.

It didn't work.

She leveled a direct gaze at him, a world of pain in her eyes. "I didn't think a convenience store on a quiet Saturday morning was, either."

His smile evaporated. Instantly. "It shouldn't have been. Which goes to prove that no matter how hard we try to protect the people we love, we don't always succeed. We can only do our best to keep them safe and then put them in God's hands."

"God fell down on the job that day." Her eyes grew hard and cold. "That's why I've taken on full responsibility for Zach's safety."

"You can't be with him every minute, Catherine." He maintained a conversational tone, tamping down any suggestion of censure. "And even if you could, he needs space to grow. And breathe. And be a kid."

Her jaw tightened, and the mutinous tilt of her chin told him she didn't like his comment. "You think I'm smothering him, don't you?"

"I think you love him with every fiber of your being. I think you want the best for him. I think you're willing to go to any length to protect him." He chose his next words with care. "But sometimes that can backfire. Too much of a good thing isn't always good."

A flame ignited in her eyes and she propped her fists on her hips. "You know, you might have a different take on this if you were in my shoes. If you'd lost someone you loved to violence. If you had an innocent, vulnerable child who counted on you to protect and nurture him. It's easy to give advice when you don't have that kind of responsibility. When you've never experienced the devastating effects of trauma on a little boy."

A cold knot formed in Nathan's gut as a surge of ugly memories snatched the breath from his lungs. It happened once in a while, after some random comment stirred that rancid pot. But this time, instead of shoving them back into a dark corner of his heart, he heard himself speaking.

"As a matter of fact, I have."

In the shocked silence that followed his reply, Catherine stared at him. But she was no more stunned than he was. He'd never even *hinted* at his dark secret to anyone. Only God was privy to it. And a man long gone from his life, whose specter could still haunt him on a bad night.

Slowly Catherine uncrossed her arms and let them drop to her sides. "Do you want to explain that?" Her tone was no longer strident, and her eyes had softened, encouraging him to confide.

He turned away abruptly. No, he didn't want to explain. The mere thought of sharing his secret filled him with disgust and self-loathing—the very emotions it had taken him years to conquer.

Walking to the window, he gripped the sill and let the vast expanse of bright blue sky and open land soothe him. What had prompted him to make that admission? To open the door to the horror he'd kept hidden for so long?

And what would Catherine think if she knew the sordid details?

Yet…if he was interested in a relationship with her, if he thought the two of them had serious potential, could he keep it a secret? *Should* he keep it a secret? Wasn't love all about trust and sharing and acceptance?

"I'm sorry I jumped all over you about Zach, Nathan." Catherine's contrite, caring voice was like a balm on his tattered soul. "But you hit a nerve. Because deep in my subconscious, I know you're right. I'm stifling him with my love, and I need to back off. I'm sure it took a lot of courage for you to bring it up, and I appreciate your insights. Sometimes someone else's take on a situation can provide a new perspective."

She was giving him an opening. Not pushing, just making herself available if he wanted to explain his comment.

And maybe it was time to put aside the shame and guilt and bring the dark secret into the light of day. Expose it to the sunlight, in all its ugliness.

But to do that, he'd have to overcome the thing that had always held him back.

Fear of rejection.

And he wasn't certain he could do that.

Even with Catherine.

Closing his eyes, he sent a plea to the Lord for guidance—and courage.

From her spot by the door, Catherine studied Nathan's broad back, her stomach clenching. His rigid posture, the flash of pain—and fear—in his eyes before he'd turned away, the tension she could feel emanating from him, told her there was a very good chance he was going to reject her overture. And she couldn't blame him. Not after the way she'd reacted when he'd broached—in a very diplomatic way—the subject of her behavior toward Zach.

Her son himself had tried to clue her in to her mistake. His comment yesterday, when she'd clung to him after he'd fallen off the fence, had said it all.

"Hey, Mom, you're squeezing me to death."

Nathan had seconded that as he'd pried her son free.

"You need to let him go, Catherine, so he can breathe."

They were both right.

Summoning up her courage, she moved behind him and laid her hand against his arm. "Nathan, I'd…"

He jerked at her touch as if he'd been struck, and she snatched her hand away, backing up a few steps. The light from the window threw his tense profile into harsh relief, and she watched his Adam's apple bob as he swallowed. Hard.

"I'm sorry. I didn't mean to startle you." She wiped her palms on her jeans.

A parade of emotions strobed across his eyes as he glanced at her. Uncertainty. Fear. Anguish. Dread. And a host of others she couldn't identify. Until at last they all gave way to an odd combination of resignation and resolve.

Shifting away from her once again, he spoke in a hollow voice she'd never heard him use before.

"My story isn't pretty, Catherine."

"Neither is mine."

"Mine could change things between us."

That scared her a little. But she already knew he was an ex-con. How much worse could it be? Unless…

"Have you…did you kill someone in your past life?" The question came out tentative. Hushed.

He gave a bitter laugh. "No. But I wanted to."

Silence fell again. As if he was giving her a chance to retract her offer to listen to his story.

Part of her wanted to back off. Avoid whatever it was Nathan was loath to reveal. But how could she do that, when she knew it had had a profound effect on this man who was fast claiming a piece of her heart?

Straightening her shoulders, she braced herself. "Tell me what happened, Nathan. Please."

Several more beats of silence ticked by. He didn't move. He didn't turn toward her. He just gave her the stark facts in a flat voice.

"I was molested as a child by my father. Repeatedly."

As his words registered, the world around them went still as death. Catherine felt as if all the air in the room was being sucked out, and the floor seemed to shift beneath her feet. A wave of nausea swept over her, and she pressed her fingertips against the wall to steady herself as the horror behind his terse words registered.

Now she understood the painting at Blue Water Gallery.

And wished she didn't.

Blinking back tears, she swallowed past the lump in her throat. She wanted to offer reassurances, tell him everything was okay. But that wasn't true. The past couldn't be undone. And it was far from okay. The only consolation she could offer was a hug, but his rigid posture discouraged trespassing.

"I told you it wasn't pretty, Catherine." He looked at her over his shoulder, his shattered expression clear evidence of the soul-crushing abuse he had suffered so many years ago.

It also propelled her forward. Closing the distance between them, she wrapped her arms around him and held him as fiercely as she'd held Zach yesterday.

For a few heartbeats he froze, as if stunned by her impulsive move. And then he lifted his own arms and pulled her close, burying his face in her hair as he clung to her.

No words were spoken.

None were needed.

Catherine didn't know how much time passed. But eventually she eased back and took his hand. Dropping down to the floor, she tugged him with her until there were sitting with their backs against the freshly painted wall in the empty room. As he drew up his knees, she angled toward him.

"How old were you when this started, Nathan?" Her question was muted, her tone gentle.

"Seven." His voice rasped as he stared at their clasped hands.

A year older than Zach.

Catherine closed her eyes and swallowed past the bile that rose in her throat. If anyone ever touched her son like that, she'd... The horror was too great to contemplate. She thrust it aside, repulsed.

Nathan drew a ragged breath, and he continued in a voice that was rough as gravel. "It went on for four years. He'd show up in my room after dinner, when I was playing or doing my homework. I got to know the pattern. He'd wait for a night that J.C. was at a Scout meeting or basketball practice. A couple of hours later he'd send my mom and Marci to the store on some trumped-up errand. Then he'd come to the room I shared with J.C. Lock the door. Close the blinds. And..." Nathan's voice broke, and he dipped his head.

Catherine swallowed, trying to vanquish the bitter taste from her mouth.

It wouldn't go away.

"Did you ever tell anyone?" She squeezed his hand, wishing she could erase the terrible memories from his mind.

His Adam's apple bobbed again. When he spoke, his words were underscored with bitterness. "No. He played all the angles to keep me quiet. He said he'd beat me if I told anyone. That the abuse was my fault. That I was a bad person. He threatened to leave if I said a word, and that if my family starved in the gutter the blame would be mine."

All at once, he started to shake. Catherine scooted closer to stroke his face, and a shudder ran through him at her touch.

"I'm surprised I haven't run you off by now." His words came out broken. Choked.

"I'm not going anywhere."

His grip on her hand tightened. "God, it was terrible." He closed his eyes, and his lashes grew spiky with moisture. "I felt so many emotions a seven-year-old should never experience. Betrayal. Guilt. Shame. And finally, anger. Since I felt like dirt, why not act like dirt? I was always in trouble in school, and once I dropped out I hooked up with a bad crowd. I drank. I experimented with drugs. I turned to crime. I was always searching for something that would make me feel important. In control. Nothing worked."

"What about your brother and sister? Did your father…"

"No. He didn't touch Marci. And from early on, it was clear to everyone that J.C. wouldn't tolerate immoral or illegal behavior. I guess that's why he became a cop. My father didn't fool with him. In his sick, twisted mind I was the chosen one." He dragged his fingers through his hair and shook his head. "I long ago gave up trying to figure out how pedophiles think."

Several beats of silence passed as Catherine processed all she'd heard. And came to the only possible conclusion.

"You know what's really remarkable?" She tightened her grip on his strong, lean fingers. "The fact that you turned into such a caring, compassionate man despite all the bad stuff in your life."

"I wouldn't have without J.C. He kept believing in me long after I stopped believing in myself and he stuck by me through everything. Thanks to him, I finally saw the light."

"What was the turning point?"

"Two years ago, I told a fellow inmate my brother was an undercover detective. That little slip blew his cover, and two men died because of it. J.C. could have been killed, too. It was the lowest point in my life. I felt like the worthless piece of trash my father always said I was. And so I…I tried to take my own life."

Catherine stopped breathing. Nathan had warned her his story was rough, but she'd had no idea.

"I blew that, too, though. And the next thing I knew, J.C. and Marci showed up. Their love gave me a reason to live. J.C. also got me started on the road to faith. And with the Lord's help—plus a lot of assistance from the chaplain—I realized there are a lot of ways to be in prison that don't involve metal bars. In time, I made my peace with the past and moved on."

As his words resonated in the empty room, Catherine tried to absorb all she'd heard. But her brain was on overload.

He captured her gaze, holding it fast as her mind whirled. "I've never told that story to anyone, Catherine. Not even J.C. or the chaplain."

He'd shared his deepest, darkest secret with her.

She'd never felt so touched—or honored—in her life.

"Are you sorry you asked?"

She heard the trepidation in his quiet question. And deep in his eyes she glimpsed the little boy he'd once been: a child hurt, afraid and uncertain, who'd expected nothing but abuse and rejection. Who'd been taught to believe he was worthless and bad.

There was only one way to convince him she didn't believe that.

Swiveling toward him, she rose on her knees and rested her hands on his shoulders. Surprise flickered across his features, but she didn't give him a chance to wonder about her intentions. Instead, she leaned over and kissed him.

Just as he'd kissed her yesterday.

It didn't take him long to respond. Gripping her

shoulders, he molded his lips to hers in an expression of gratitude and caring so powerful and heartfelt it left her breathless.

When at last he released her, she could feel him trembling.

"Thank you for sharing all that with me, Nathan. I'm honored," she whispered.

His gaze caressed her face, and the warmth in his eyes now looked a whole lot more like love than gratitude. Her heart skipped a beat.

"Thank you for accepting me despite all the bad stuff."

"That bad stuff is part of what made you who you are today."

He grimaced. "I wish there'd been an easier way to get here."

"I do, too."

Squeezing her fingers, he checked his watch and sighed. Then he rose and gave her a hand up. "I need to get to my other job. Will I see you at church Sunday?"

"We'll be there. I have some fence-mending to do with the Lord, too."

He smiled and touched her cheek. "Thank you again… for everything."

Striding across the room, he pushed through the door and disappeared around the front of the house.

For a long while after he left, Catherine remained

in the empty room he'd restored with such meticulous care. Just as he'd restored her life.

All at once, a heartening wave of hope washed over her. If he could build a new life after all the damage that had been inflicted on him, surely she could find the courage to do the same.

And if she was very lucky, perhaps that life could include the man who'd befriended Zach—and was fast becoming much more than a friend to Zach's mom.

Chapter Eleven

As Nathan stepped outside the church on Sunday, he scanned the crowd on the lawn. In seconds he picked Catherine out. She was off to one side. Digging through her purse. Looking gorgeous.

A slow smile curved his lips. The rays of sun peeking through the trees gilded the honey-colored highlights in her hair, and her silky, teal-green blouse and black pencil skirt flattered her slender figure.

His appreciative perusal was interrupted by a chuckle from behind him, followed by a gentle shove.

"You're creating a roadblock, dear brother."

Marci's amused voice brought a surge of heat to his neck, and he quickly moved out of the path of traffic.

She was right on his heels. "You better go catch

her before she gets away—or some other guy snags her attention."

He hesitated. Although that had been his plan, following through on it now would only verify Marci's assumption that he was interested in Catherine. And that, in turn, would lead to more ribbing.

"What are you waiting for?" She planted her hands on her hips and tipped her head. "It's obvious you find her attractive. So go for it."

He strove for a casual stance, all the while keeping Catherine in his peripheral vision. She was walking around the side of the church. Alone. Had she let Zach attend Sunday school? Was she going to retrieve him? Would he have a chance to talk with her before she took off?

"Why are you so bent on marrying me off, anyway?" he replied distractedly.

One of Marci's eyebrows arched. "Did I say anything about marriage?"

The heat on his neck surged past his collar. He'd walked right into that one.

She folded her arms across her chest and gave him a smug look. "This is more serious than I thought. What do you think, Christopher?"

As her new husband joined her, he grinned and draped an arm around her shoulders. "I plead the Fifth."

"Coward," she grumbled.

He tugged her closer. "I will add one thing, though. He who hesitates…" He lifted one shoulder and winked at Nathan. "Come on, Marci. Your brother doesn't need our help to go after what he wants."

"I'm not sure about that. You and I are going to have a long talk later," she called over her shoulder as Christopher took her hand and tugged her the other direction.

Ignoring his sister's parting comment, Nathan strode across the lawn, heading in the direction Catherine had disappeared.

As he rounded the corner of the building, he saw her emerging from a side door, Zach's hand in hers. As she stepped outside, a young mother exited behind her, the little boy Zach had talked with after the service last week by her side.

"Excuse me…"

At the woman's summons, Catherine angled toward her.

Nathan slowed his steps, but was close enough to hear the exchange.

"I was hoping to catch you and introduce myself. I'm Lauren Douglas, and this is Adam." She smiled and rested her hand on the youngster's shoulder. "Our sons met last week."

Catherine returned the woman's smile. "I'm Catherine Walker. And this is Zach."

"Nice to meet you both. Are you new on the island?"

"Yes. We've only been here since early May."

"Well, welcome to Nantucket—and to our church. I'm having a birthday party this Tuesday for Adam, and I've invited all the children in his Sunday-school class. Zach would be very welcome. We're going to have pizza and hot dogs at the house and play a few games."

Nathan noted Zach's eager expression as the little boy cast a pleading look up at Catherine.

"Can I go, Mom?"

She hesitated. Nathan watched her moisten lips. Swallow. Straighten her shoulders. "Yes. Thank you for inviting him."

Withdrawing an invitation from her purse, the other woman handed it over. "All the details are on this, but call if you have any questions. We'll look forward to seeing Zach."

The two little boys grinned at each other as Lauren ushered her son toward the street.

"This is so cool, Mom!" Zach hopped from one foot to the other, unable to contain his excitement. "Hey, Nathan!" He waved as he caught sight of his older buddy. "I'm going to a party!"

A becoming flush tinted Catherine's cheeks as she turned toward him. Taking Zach's hand, she crossed the lawn.

"I heard, champ." Zach tousled the little boy's hair, but his focus was on Catherine. "That was a big step." He smiled his approval,

Her flush deepened, but her gaze didn't waver. "It was time."

"Good morning!"

At the cheery greeting, Nathan turned toward his landlady's familiar voice. She was huffing a bit as she bustled up to them after making a quick detour to her car, an oversized purse in one hand and a plate of homemade cinnamon rolls in the other. Her husband, Chester, whose ornery cowlick had—as usual—refused to be subdued despite a generous application of hair gel, followed a few steps behind.

"My dear, I've seen you at services and have been meaning to introduce myself. I'm Edith Shaw and this is my husband, Chester." She gestured over her shoulder, and the older man gave a shy dip of his head. "Hello, Nathan."

"Good morning. Edith and Chester own the cottage I'm living in," Nathan explained to Catherine.

"Nice to meet you both. I'm Catherine Walker, and this is my son, Zach."

"I've noticed Zach during services. A fine, handsome young lad." Edith smiled down at him, and he beamed back. "I thought you and your mom might like some cinnamon rolls. They always perk up a Sunday morning." She winked at Zach and handed the plate to Catherine.

"Those look really good!" Zach watched with interest as the plate transferred hands. "Thank you!"

"You're very welcome." The older woman turned her attention back to Catherine. "How's the inn coming along?" When Catherine gave her a surprised look, she chuckled. "My dear, it's a small island. Becky and I are in the garden club. Since she handles real estate all over the island, she's always a good one for news."

After living in Edith's backyard for almost six weeks, Nathan was used to her full-speed-ahead style, but Catherine hadn't yet gotten her sea legs. He stepped in to help.

"The inn is coming along great. I can guarantee it will be ready to welcome its first visitors in August."

"I'm not surprised. I've heard good things about your skills. Such a talented man." Edith shook her head. "You know he paints, of course. Pictures, that is, not walls." She gave Catherine a keen look.

"Yes."

"Ah." A satisfied smile lit her face, and she shot a meaningful glance in Nathan's direction as she tapped the plate of goodies. "There are plenty of cinnamon rolls to share, my dear. And if ever you need a sitter, don't hesitate to call. I love kids. I watch my neighbors' two girls, and in the not-too-distant future I'll be watching this one's new niece or nephew." She gestured toward Nathan.

J.C. and Heather hadn't told him about the day care arrangements for their imminent arrival, but he wasn't surprised. From what he'd seen, Edith was a natural with kids. And she lived just two houses down from The Devon Rose. What could be more perfect?

"Thank you. I'll keep that in mind," Catherine replied.

"You do that. Well, we're off. Nice to meet you both." Snagging Chester's arm, she barreled toward a small group across the lawn, towing her husband in her wake.

"Do you feel as if a hurricane just passed through?" Catherine stared after the departing duo.

"She's a bundle of energy, that's for sure," Nathan observed.

"You want to come back to our house and have some cinnamon rolls, Nathan? That lady said there was enough to share," Zach piped up.

Indeed she had, Nathan reflected. The Lighthouse Lane matchmaker had struck again.

"You'd be welcome to join us, Nathan," Catherine seconded.

And scored a hit, it seemed.

He fought down a surge of regret. "I'd like to. But I promised to have brunch with J.C. and Heather, and I've already stood them up once since I've been here."

The flash of disappointment in Catherine's eyes warmed his heart.

"We'll see you tomorrow, then." She took Zach's hand again.

"I'll be there."

"See ya, Nathan," Zach called over his shoulder as they started across the grass.

He lifted a hand in farewell, then shoved it into his pocket as he watched them strike off down the street toward their car.

When he turned, he found both Edith and Marci watching him from afar—with a gleam in their eyes. It was clear they both thought there was potential with him and Catherine.

He hoped they were right.

And if the intervention of his nosy sister and the Lighthouse Lane matchmaker helped him realize that potential, he didn't mind their interference in the least.

Catherine took a sip of coffee, picked up her pen and stared at the blank sheet of paper in front of her. With Zach down for his nap, quiet had descended in the house. Sated with cinnamon rolls and worn out from a long walk on the beach spent chasing seagulls and collecting shells, he'd fallen into bed with nary a protest. That meant she had at least an hour or two to tackle the most difficult letter she'd ever had to write.

A letter to the man who'd killed her husband.

Two months ago, if anyone had told her she'd ever reach this point, she'd have consigned them to the loony farm. Stop despising the man who'd destroyed her world? Give up the hate that had fueled her days and overpowered her grief, subduing it to a manageable level? No way.

But a lot had changed in the past five weeks.

Thanks to Nathan.

Not yet ready to begin her difficult task, she set her pen aside and wrapped her hands around her mug, letting its heat permeate her fingers—much as Nathan had infused her life with warmth.

For with his kind and gentle ways, he'd demolished her conviction that no criminal could be rehabilitated. By showing her the power of faith to transform a life, he'd inspired her to take the first steps toward reconnecting with the Lord. And his successful efforts to make peace with his horrendous past and move beyond it had convinced her she, too, could create something good out of the ashes of her old life.

But to do that, she had to dispel her hate once and for all. She had to acknowledge that while the act that had stolen her husband's life was wrong, the man who had done it could have been as misguided and abused as Nathan had been. While that didn't excuse his crime, Nathan's experience had given her a better understanding of how forces beyond a person's control could twist and deform a life.

Yesterday had been a turning point for her. Not only because Nathan had shared his terrible story. But because of what he'd said near the end.

There are a lot of ways to be in prison that don't involve metal bars.

That one sentence had struck a chord deep within her.

For she'd been living in a prison of a different kind these past two years. Hate and fear had isolated her from God and from life. She'd clung to Zach, seeing him as the only good thing in her world, smothering him with her attention, burdening him by making him her sole source of joy.

That hadn't been fair. To either of them.

Zach was antsy to spread his wings. To broaden the scope of his world.

It was time she did the same.

But first she had to begin the process of bringing closure to the trauma from her past.

Based on her faith, she acknowledged that for-giveness had to be her ultimate goal. She wasn't there yet. Not even close. But she was ready to take the first step in that direction. Because the fact that her husband's killer had sent her a letter suggested he might have a conscience after all. Perhaps something had enlightened him to the error of his ways, imbued him with guilt and a sense of remorse.

Perhaps he was finding his way to the Lord, in much the same way Nathan had.

If so, a letter from her might speed his journey—just as Nathan's quiet faith had helped her begin her own journey of reconnecting to the Almighty.

She closed her eyes. Folded her hands on the table. Bowed her head.

Lord, please soften my heart. Give me the words that will accomplish Your will and bring this lost soul back to You. Guide my hand and my heart as I take this first painful step toward forgiveness. And fill me with courage and trust in Your goodness as I prepare to let go of the past and embrace the future You have planned for me.

Taking a deep breath, she picked up her pen and began to write.

On Wednesday afternoon, as Nathan braked to a stop on his bicycle in front of Catherine's house, the sound of violin music wafted through the quiet air, as it had a few weeks ago. But what a change from the last impromptu concert he'd overheard.

Resting his bike against the split-rail fence, he took a few moments to enjoy the lilting, upbeat classical piece. In direct contrast to the previous melody, this one brimmed with optimism and lightheartedness.

It sounded the way he felt.

Thanks to the past three days.

As they'd worked side by side to lay the flooring in the remodeled rooms, their relationship had evolved into an easy, natural, comfortable camaraderie. A hurdle had been vaulted, barriers dismantled. Nathan suspected some of the change was due to the story he'd shared with her last Friday. But Catherine had also told him about the letter she'd written to her husband's killer—the first, freeing step toward forgiveness and a future unencumbered by the past.

There was another very significant change, as well.

She'd taken off her wedding ring.

That's what had given him the courage to ask her—and Zach—out on a date.

Unless it failed him before he issued the invitation.

The music ceased, and Nathan took that as his cue to head toward the breezeway.

Zach must have been watching for him, because the youngster banged through the door the instant he stepped inside, his face animated, his greeting enthusiastic.

"Hey, Nathan."

"Hi, champ."

"Mom's got something to ask you."

"Yeah?"

"Let me get her." He grinned and raced back inside.

Half a minute later, the two of them emerged again, Zach tugging on Catherine's hand. Her color was a little higher than usual, and Nathan gave her a curious look. "What's up?"

She tucked her hair behind her ear. Shifted from one foot to the other. "Well…you probably already have plans, and it's okay if you do. I know you have family on the island, and I'm sure they'd like to spend the day with you. So don't feel obligated." She folded her arms across her chest. Swallowed. "But the thing is…we were wondering…" She paused and cleared her throat.

Zach huffed out an exasperated breath and cut to the chase. "Do you want to have a picnic with us and go see fireworks on the Fourth of July?"

A slow smile curved Nathan's lips as a blush crept up Catherine's cheeks. "That's funny. I was going to ask you guys the same thing."

"Honest?" Enthusiasm lit Zach's eyes.

"Honest." He kept his gaze fixed on Catherine's. "I can't think of anyone I'd rather celebrate my independence with."

The warmth of her smile chased away the last lingering chill from the darkest corner of his soul.

"Oh, boy! This will be so much fun!" Zach hopped from one foot to the other, unable to contain his excitement. "Isn't this great, Mom?"

Her smile deepened, producing an endearing dimple on one side of her mouth that he'd never noticed before. "Yeah. It is. We'll talk about the details after we finish the floor." She started toward the rooms on the other side of the breezeway. "I know you have another job to go to this afternoon, so we'd better…"

He snagged her arm as she passed, and she stopped. When she looked at him, the pulse fluttering in the hollow of her throat tripped his own heart into double time, and it took every ounce of his willpower to restrain the urge to kiss her. That would have to wait for a private moment.

"Thank you." He said the words softly, for her ears only. Expressing gratitude for far more than a simple outing.

And she knew it. He could tell by the way her eyes softened with tenderness. And by the gentle, unexpected brush of her lips against his cheek as she stood on tiptoe, then moved on.

Leaving him with a silly grin on his face that he was pretty certain matched the one on Zach's.

Chapter Twelve

"What're you looking for, Mom?"

Sparing Zach a quick, distracted glance, Catherine continued to search the kitchen. "I left some money here this morning, but now I can't find it." Eight fifty-dollar bills she'd gotten from the ATM last night, to be exact. And she was certain she'd set the envelope containing the cash on the kitchen counter. That's what she usually did when she got home from running errands.

Truth be told, though, she hadn't been thinking very straight over the past few days—thanks to a certain visitor with velvet-brown eyes who'd been playing havoc with her metabolism. "Did you see a white envelope anywhere out here, Zach?"

"Nope." He propped his elbow on the table and took a big bite of his chocolate-chip cookie. "Why don't you ask Nathan? He came in to get a bandage for my finger while you were on your cell phone in the backyard. I got a splinter. It bled a little, but he fixed it for me." Her son held up his latex-wrapped pinkie. "Maybe he saw the money."

Nathan had entered the house uninvited? That was a first. But now that he'd witnessed Zach's reaction to blood, she could understand his quick response to even a minor injury. And she *had* been on the phone for an extended period with her sister. He probably hadn't wanted to interrupt her.

Zach was right. It was possible he'd seen the money.

Or taken it.

Shocked by that unbidden thought, her eyes widened. Where in the world had *that* come from? Of course he hadn't taken the money! Nathan wasn't hurting for cash. He had more jobs than he could handle, and he'd just sold a painting for an impressive price. Why would he take a few hundred dollars from her?

Because stealing is in his blood.

No!

Catherine gripped the edge of the counter, steadying herself. Why were such hateful thoughts darting through her mind, leaving suspicion and agitation in their wake, disrupting her equilibrium, dimming the joy that had lifted her heart of late?

Nathan had changed. He wasn't a thief anymore. He was a kind, caring, generous man with high morals and rock-solid principles. And he'd proven that to her in every way humanly possible, demonstrating that her once-a-criminal, always-a-criminal stereotype had been wrong, wrong, wrong.

So why was it rearing its ugly head now? After she thought she'd put it rest for good?

It was unforgivable. And it made her feel awful.

"Do you have a tummy ache, Mom?"

At Zach's question, she tightened her grip on the counter. "No, honey. Why do you ask?"

"Your face looks funny. Like something hurts."

Something did. Her conscience.

Pasting on a smile, she released her grip on the counter and topped off his glass of milk. "I'm fine, Zach. Now finish up that cookie. It's naptime."

Summoning up every bit of her resolve, she pushed aside her noxious suspicions. She wasn't going to let doubt infiltrate and destroy the relationship she was building with Nathan. She wasn't. That would be a huge mistake—one she suspected she'd regret for the rest of her life. The money had to be around the house somewhere. The place had been chaotic ever since the move, and she might have set it down in another room without thinking.

It would turn up. She was sure of it. And until it did, she was determined to banish every last doubt about Nathan from her mind.

Zach rested his chin in his hand. "I could help you look for your money, Mom."

A genuine grin tugged at her lips, replacing her artificial smile. Her son would try anything to get out of taking a nap. "I appreciate the offer, honey. But I can handle it."

She retrieved the dishcloth from the sink and joined Zach at the table. Crumbs were scattered over the surface, and she wiped them up into a neat pile and disposed of them.

Vowing yet again to do the same with the unwelcome, insidious crumbs of suspicion that were cluttering her mind.

"You do great work, Nathan. I can't even tell where the hole used to be."

Balanced on one knee, he continued to apply the final coat of cream-colored paint to the wall of the family room in the palatial, ocean-front home where he'd been working for the past three days. And did his best to discreetly put some distance between himself and Danielle Price.

But she only leaned farther over, her long hair swinging close enough to brush his face as she pretended to examine his work.

He had to bite his tongue to keep from telling her to back off.

If he hadn't been loath to leave a job unfinished, and if this hadn't been his last visit, he wouldn't be here today. The twenty-something blonde made him nervous. Big-time. He'd met her fiftyish husband on his first visit, as the man was leaving their summer home for a fishing excursion, and this woman had bored trophy wife written all over her. Worse, she was on the prowl.

He didn't intend to be her prey.

"Thanks." He continued to stroke the paint over the repair he'd made in the drywall, feathering it out with a light touch so it would blend seamlessly into the existing paint, hurrying as much as he could without compromising the quality of his work.

"Can I hand you a tool or anything?" She moved in again and leaned a shoulder against the undamaged part of the wall. Shoving her hands into the pockets of her micro-shorts, she exposed a broad section of midriff under her low-cut cropped top. Right at his eye level.

Nathan swallowed past his distaste and did his best to ignore the flagrant flirting.

"No, thanks, Mrs. Price. I'm about finished here."

She gave him a little pout he suspected she was used to employing to her advantage. He supposed some men might find it appealing. It had the opposite effect on him.

"Now, Nathan. I told you to call me Danielle. We don't have to be so formal."

"I always show respect to my customers." He added a few more strokes, stood and stepped back. It was good enough. "Okay. That should do it. I'll go clean my brush and get out of your hair."

He started to turn away, but she startled him by snagging one of the belt loops on his jeans with a perfectly manicured finger. When he looked back at her, she gave him a sultry smile. "I wouldn't mind having you in my hair, Nathan."

Disgusted by the blatant come-on, he extricated himself and eased away. "I'm sure Mr. Price wouldn't be too happy to hear that."

She gave an indifferent shrug. "He's gone all the time. When we're in Boston, he's at the office. When we're here, he fishes. A girl can get lonely." She sidled up to him, her baby blues locked on his lips, her tone seductive. "But you know all about being lonely, don't you, Nathan? I hear prison is a very lonely place."

He sucked in a sharp breath and stared at her, blindsided.

A smug smile lifted her lips. "It's amazing how much you can learn by searching about a person on Google, isn't it?"

Repulsed, he took another step back. "You checked me out on the Internet?"

She lifted one shoulder. "Why not? I always search the Internet about things I'm interested in."

His back stiffened. "I don't appreciate having my privacy invaded."

She gave a careless shrug. "Your incarceration is public record, Nathan. But that's beside the point." She moved in again and rested her fingers against his chest. "The fact is, my husband is gone. You're lonely. I'm lonely. The way I keep score, that equals a pair."

Very deliberately, he removed her hand from his T-shirt. Until now, he'd tried to be polite. This time he made no attempt to warm up the chill in his voice. "Not to me. I don't play those kinds of games. And for the record, I'm not lonely. Excuse me while I take care of this brush."

He turned, but not before he caught the sudden bright spots of color in her cheeks. Apparently his customer wasn't used to having her advances rejected.

His conclusion was verified when he returned to the family room and found her lounging in a rattan chair, paging through a magazine. Her pose was nonchalant, but the cobalt eyes she strafed him with were cold enough to stave off global warming. As was her tone.

"Your toolboxes are in the foyer. Pull the door shut behind you when you leave."

Without a word, Nathan exited the room. After retrieving the twin boxes, he let himself out and stowed them in the wire baskets on the back of his bike. Then he mounted and took off as fast as he could.

Leaving behind his first unsatisfied customer.

And feeling nothing but relief.

"Hi, Nathan!"

As he biked up the dirt road toward Sheltering Shores Inn the next morning, Nathan grinned at Zach's boisterous welcome. The youngster was peeking through the split-rail fence that separated the yard from the road, and he gave a vigorous wave.

Returning the gesture, Nathan pulled to a stop. "Hi, champ. What are you doing out here?"

"Mom said I could come out and watch for you."

He glanced toward the house and spotted Catherine at the window, half-hidden behind the drapes. She was obviously still fighting the protective instincts that compelled her to keep a too-tight tether on Zach. But he gave her high marks for making an effort to subdue them. As far as he knew, she'd never let Zach go into the front yard alone. This was a big step forward.

As he leaned the bike against the rails, Nathan

reached into the wire basket behind the seat and withdrew a white bag. "Guess where I stopped?"

Zach's eyes lit up. "Downyflake!"

"You got it." He handed the bag over.

"Wow! Doughnuts and cake all in one day!"

"Isn't ten o'clock a little early for cake?"

"I haven't had any yet. Mom baked it for our wrap party. She says you're gonna finish today. By lunch, maybe?"

"That sounds about right." All he had to do was plane one sticky door and readjust a couple of baseboards that didn't quite suit him. Other than that, the rooms were finished, giving Catherine three weeks to furnish and decorate them before her first guests were due to arrive.

Retrieving his toolboxes, he set off for the breezeway. Catherine was waiting inside with a smile that brightened his day despite the dark clouds beginning to gather overhead.

"I see you brought a treat." She gestured to the white bag clutched in Zach's hand.

"I hear you made a cake."

"Sounds like we both have celebrations on our minds."

The soft blush that accompanied her words was charming. And so much more appealing than the in-your-face come-on moves Danielle had tried on him yesterday.

Pushing the memory of that distasteful episode aside, he headed for the guest room on the left. "I don't think it will take me more than an hour or two to finish up. Then we can get down to the important stuff. Like partying. Right, Zach?"

"Yeah!" Digging into the white sack, he extracted a sugar doughnut. "Is it okay if I have one of these now, though, Mom?"

"Sure. But in the kitchen. On a plate. I don't want sugar all over my pristine guest quarters."

"What's pristine?"

She ushered him toward the kitchen. "Clean."

"Oh." He gave up the fight and trotted toward the door, calling over his shoulder as Catherine guided him inside. "I'll be out to help in a few minutes, Nathan."

"Okay, champ."

Five minutes later, when Nathan heard a noise behind him, he assumed it was Zach. But checking over his shoulder, he found Catherine instead. Her smile had vanished, and two parallel creases had appeared on her brow. A tingle of alarm raced up his spine, and he stood.

"What's wrong?" He took a step toward her. "Is Zach okay?"

"Yes." She gestured over her shoulder. "But there's a police detective out front. He says he's your brother."

J.C. was here?

Now it was his turn to frown. "What does he want?"

"I don't know. He just asked to talk with you."

"Okay." Nathan set down the hammer he'd been holding, his concern escalating. Maybe something had happened to Marci. Or Heather might be having problems with the baby that was due in six weeks. Or…

Quashing his useless speculations, he eased past Catherine, laying a reassuring hand briefly on her shoulder. Then he cut through the breezeway and exited onto the front lawn. J.C. was waiting by his car, and he closed the distance between them in a few long strides.

"What's up? Is everyone okay?"

"Yeah. We're all fine. But I need to talk to you about a situation that came up this morning."

At J.C.'s somber demeanor and grim tone, a flicker of panic licked at Nathan's gut. Just like the ones he used to feel when the law was closing in on him.

Something bad was about to come down. He could taste it.

A tremor ran through him.

J.C.'s eyes narrowed and he took a step closer. "What's wrong?"

Every instinct in Nathan's body screamed at him

to run. It took a Herculean exercise of willpower to keep his feet planted on the ground. "You tell me. You might be my brother, but I've been around cops enough to know when there's a problem."

Resting one fist on his hip, J.C. raked the fingers of his other hand through his hair. "I need to ask you a few questions, okay?"

"As a brother or as a cop?"

J.C. locked gazes with him. "Let's be clear on one thing, Nathan. As a brother, I know there's a reasonable explanation for what happened. But as a cop, I have a job to do. One of the other detectives should be handling this, but the chief and I go way back. He agreed to let me talk to you before this thing gets blown out of proportion."

"What thing?"

"Where were you yesterday afternoon?"

"In Monomoy. At the Prices'. Finishing up a job."

"Who was there?"

Nathan tried not to let his distaste show on his face. "Danielle Price."

"Anyone else?"

"No."

"Did you see a diamond tennis bracelet lying on the table in the family room?"

"No."

"Mrs. Price claims it was there yesterday afternoon. Now it's not. She says the only person who's been in the house other than her and her husband since she noticed it missing is you."

As the implication sank in, Nathan's lungs froze. Early on, he'd pegged Danielle Price as a spoiled socialite who was used to getting her own way. And he knew she'd been angry when he'd rebuffed her advances.

But the viciousness of her retaliation boggled his mind. From what she'd learned about him from searching the Internet, she'd known exactly how to make him pay for his offense. With his record, the police would not only consider him the prime suspect in the supposed theft, they'd *assume* he'd taken it.

Nathan's shock gave way to escalating anger. But before it swelled to fury, a far stronger emotion elbowed it aside.

Terror.

Given his record, this woman could make his life miserable. Maybe even get him sent back to prison.

A wave of nausea swept over him, and he started to shake.

Twin grooves appeared on J.C.'s brow. Stepping close, he grasped Nathan's upper arms in a firm, steadying grip. "Take a deep breath."

He tried. But his lungs wouldn't cooperate. "I didn't…steal it, J.C."

"I believe you."

"No one else will. J.C., I can't go back to prison." He choked out the words. The mere thought of being confined again in a cage was enough to take the stiffening out of his legs. "I can't!"

"Don't worry about that, okay? Everything's going to be fine."

Pulling him into a bear hug, J.C. held on tight. Just as Catherine had done with Zach after his accident.

But as Nathan had told Catherine once, no matter how hard you try to protect the ones you love, you don't always succeed. In the end, you have to put them in God's hands.

And his instincts told him that in this situation, it might take God to put things right.

From her spot in the breezeway, Catherine shivered as she watched the scene playing out in her front yard.

Something was very wrong.

Uncertainty gnawing at her, she wrapped her arms around herself and debated her options. Should she leave the two men alone, stay out of an exchange that might be none of her business? Or should she *make* it her business because she cared about Nathan and it was obvious he needed support—and perhaps comfort?

In the end, J.C.'s bear hug gave her the impetus to get involved. Even from a distance, she could tell it was the kind of gesture reserved for grave emergencies.

Checking on Zach, who'd wandered into the empty guest room where Nathan had been working, she pushed through the door and headed in their direction.

Nathan's back was to her as she approached, but J.C. saw her coming. With a quiet word to his brother, followed by one more strong squeeze, he backed off a couple of steps.

"I'm sorry...I don't mean to intrude." She stopped a few feet away. "I couldn't hear what you were saying from the house, but it looked serious and I wondered if...is there anything I can do to help?"

Nathan lifted his arm and brushed the sleeve of his T-shirt across his eyes before he turned to her.

The devastation on his face drove the breath from her lungs, and she took an involuntary step forward as panic gripped her heart. "Nathan... what's wrong?"

He shoved his hands into his pockets and stared at the dirt beneath his feet. "The woman I was working for yesterday afternoon reported a stolen diamond bracelet. She said I was the only stranger in the house since she'd last seen it."

Shock reverberated through her as the implications registered. "Is she accusing you of taking it?"

"Not directly." J.C. spoke up.

Confused, she looked at him. "Are you arresting him?"

"No. I'm investigating."

"Look, J.C., you can search my cottage if you want to," Nathan interjected, his voice shaking. "Whatever it takes. Just tell me the best way to…"

"Hey, Nathan!" Zach banged through the screen door in the breezeway and bounded toward them. "How come this is in your toolbox?"

Dangling from his hand was a diamond tennis bracelet.

Catherine felt the bottom drop out of her stomach.

For a long moment, the silence was broken only by a distant, ominous rumble of thunder. Then J.C. stepped forward. "Let me take a look at that, son. I'm Nathan's brother."

His voice was taut as the strings on her violin. And the word *solemn* didn't do justice to the gravity of his expression. Catherine suppressed another shiver.

But it was Nathan who drew her attention. All the color had drained from his face, leaving shock and disbelief in its place.

J.C. lowered himself to Zach's level and inspected the bracelet in the youngster's hand. Then he pulled a small plastic bag from his pocket and held it out. "Drop it in here for me, okay?"

After her son complied, he moved beside her, suddenly subdued. No surprise there. The tense vibes surrounding the little group huddled on the lawn were almost palpable.

Moving back to Nathan, J.C. held up the bag. "Any idea how this got there?"

"I can guess."

"Okay."

"Danielle Price put it in there when I went to clean my paintbrush."

"Why would she do that?"

Nathan shot Zach a quick glance. "Let's just say she had another—more personal—job in mind for me. I wasn't interested. She wasn't happy." His carefully chosen words were terse. Clipped. "She also knows about…where I was before I came here. Courtesy of Google."

More silence.

"Mom?"

At the tentative question and the tug on her shirt, Catherine shifted her attention to Zach.

"What's wrong? Why is everybody mad?" His voice came out small and uncertain.

"We're not mad, honey. We're…concerned about something that got lost."

"Like the money in the envelope you were looking for yesterday?"

At Zach's comment, both men jerked their heads her direction.

"What money?" J.C. demanded.

Catherine's gaze flicked to Nathan. "I...uh...got some cash from the ATM and I...can't find it."

She knew this new information wasn't going to help Nathan's case. The coincidence was enough to instill doubt in anyone.

Including her...much to her disgust.

She tried to suppress it. Tried to erect barriers against it. But it was as insidious and relentless as the tide. Uncertainty crept into her consciousness—and her eyes.

And she knew the instant Nathan discerned it.

What little color was left in his face vanished, and his own eyes grew bleak.

Catherine wanted to cry.

In his moment of trial, when he'd most needed the people he cared about to support him—and believe in him—she'd let him down as badly as if she'd come right out and accused him of stealing.

"I'm heading back to the station." J.C. pocketed the bracelet, ignoring the dynamics between her and his brother. "I'm going to ask one of the other detectives to pay a visit to the Prices' and have a little talk with the lady of the house. Leave your cell on, okay?"

Breaking eye contact with her at last, Nathan focused on J.C. "Okay. Look…do you need me to go in with you?"

There was a mixture of dread and fear in his voice, and Catherine's heart ached for him.

"No. I know how to reach you." His mouth thinned and his voice grew hard. "We're not going to let her get away with this, Nathan. It's all circumstantial evidence."

"That may be all it takes for someone like me." There was quiet anguish in his tone. And defeat.

"Hey…" J.C. laid a hand on his shoulder, his tone firm. "Don't give up. We're going to beat this."

"I hope so."

"Count on it." Giving his brother's shoulder a squeeze, J.C. nodded toward her and walked toward his car.

They watched in silence as he slid in. Started the engine. Put the car in gear.

Nathan didn't speak until his brother was nothing more than a cloud of dust in the road.

"I need to go, too, Catherine."

"No." She took a step toward him. "Please stay. I'm sorry for…" Her words trailed off.

"Doubting me?" He attempted to smile, but the twist of his lips didn't even come close. "I don't know why I expected more. I'm an ex-con. But for the record, I didn't take your money."

"I know that."

"Do you?"

She deserved that. Nevertheless, his words ripped a hole in her heart.

Before she could think of a response, he moved toward his bike.

"Are you leaving, Nathan?"

Zach's question stopped him. Angling toward the little boy, a fresh wave of pain swept across his eyes. "Yeah, I am."

"What about our party?"

"I'm not real hungry for cake right now. You and your mom have the party without me, okay?"

"It won't be the same."

"I'm sorry, Zach. I can't stay."

His voice rasped, and all at once Zach pulled from her grasp and ran toward him. Nathan knelt to meet him, wrapping him in a bear hug as his shattered gaze connected with hers. There was a world of hurt in his eyes. Of betrayal. And an infinite sadness that told her the precious thing that had been within her grasp might be gone forever.

The hole in her heart widened. She felt the pressure of tears behind her eyes, in her throat, and a feeling of desperation swept over her. She couldn't let him leave like this.

Taking a step forward, she held out her hand in an imploring gesture. "Please, Nathan. I…"

He shook his head, cutting her off. "Let it go, Catherine."

It's too late.

He didn't say the words, but she saw the message in his eyes. Although she tried to stop it, a tear spilled over her lashes and trailed down her cheek.

Nathan's features contorted as he watched her, as if he, too, was fighting back tears. For one brief instant, she thought he was going to relent and forgive her. That he was going to draw her into the circle of his arms with Zach and hold her close.

But he didn't. Instead, he looked away. Then, with one final squeeze for Zach, he released her son and mounted his bike. And as he set off down the road, the gray clouds gathering above snuffed out the sun, leaving the world in shadows.

Reminding Catherine of the terrible truth of Zach's words.

It wouldn't be the same without Nathan.

Chapter Thirteen

How could things have gone so wrong so quickly?

This morning he'd been on top of the world, looking forward to a future that seemed bright and promising.

Now he was facing the very real possibility of more time behind bars.

Leaning forward in the pew he'd occupied every Sunday since he'd arrived on Nantucket, Nathan rested his elbows on his knees, dropped his head into his hands…and fought back the urge to throw up.

Though that would be a fitting conclusion to his miserable day.

Danielle Price's insinuation that he'd stolen her bracelet had been bad enough. That alone had sent raw terror drumming through his veins. After the past eight weeks of freedom, the mere *prospect* of returning to prison was sufficient to cut him off at the knees.

But the doubt in Catherine's eyes had been worse.

He massaged his brow, trying to knead away the ache pounding in his temples. As lethally as a sharp knife could slice through a carotid artery and sever the flow of blood that kept a body alive, her lack of trust in him had severed the emotional connection between them that had given his soul—and his heart—new life over these past few weeks.

How could she have any misgivings about his honesty, after all the hours they'd spent together and the closeness that had developed between them? How could she turn away from him after the secrets he'd shared with her about his past—and his hopes for the future? How could she mistrust him after she'd taken refuge in the shelter of his arms?

Her reaction had blindsided him. Left him reeling.

And raised another agonizing question.

If she couldn't believe in him in light of the view he'd given her into his soul, how could he ever expect anyone else to give him the benefit of the doubt? To have faith in him?

The answer was as simple as it was depressing.

He couldn't.

It was time to face the truth. His dream of escaping his past, of starting over, of building a new life, had been only that. A dream. The stigma of his mistakes would haunt him forever.

Nathan had no idea how long he sat in the Lord's house, seeking consolation and guidance. But the comfort he usually found in prayer eluded him. His soul felt as dry and parched as the prison toast he'd choked down for ten long years.

Rising at last, he trudged to the door and stepped outside, pausing on the small porch. The dark clouds had rolled in, and heavy rain had begun to fall. Yet above the clouds, out of sight, he knew the sun continued to shine.

Faith was like that, he reminded himself as he raised his face to the heavens. Even during life's darkest, stormiest challenges, the Lord's love and grace remained steady and strong. They might not always be apparent. Sometimes they might seem absent altogether. Like today. But he believed they were there. With every fiber of his being, he believed.

So he'd hit a rough patch. Hadn't he told Catherine not long ago that at some point, after you've done everything possible to bring about a certain result, you have to put it in God's hands?

He needed to follow his own advice.

He needed to give it to God.

And it wasn't as if he was facing this crisis alone, he reminded himself, watching the rain pummel the ground around him. There were people on his side who believed in him. J.C., for one. His brother had gone out on a limb for him today. First, by convincing his boss to let him handle the initial inquiry. And second, by letting him walk away after the bracelet turned up in his toolbox.

J.C. could have hauled him in to the station. Probably *should* have hauled him in. Instead, he'd put himself on the line, bought Nathan some breathing space. Because he didn't believe his brother was a thief—despite blatant evidence to the contrary. It was yet another example of the kind of rock-solid love J.C. had always shown for him.

No matter what happened, Nathan took some measure of comfort and consolation in knowing he could rely on that love. Both J.C. and Marci would stand by him. Catherine might harbor doubts, but his siblings never would.

And hard as it was to swallow, he supposed it was better to discover Catherine's lack of confidence in him now rather than later. What if things had progressed, gotten serious, and he'd…

The jarring ring of his cell phone interrupted his thoughts, and his pulse skyrocketed. Hands shaking, he fumbled as he extracted it from his pocket and tapped the talk button. "Hello."

"Nathan, it's J.C. Where are you?"

His heart began to pound, and he gripped the

railing around the porch. "I stopped in at church."
Please, God, let there be some good news!

"Then you might want to say a prayer of thanks. Because you're off the hook."

Closing his eyes, he lowered himself to the wooden floor and propped his back against the wall. Sucked in a lungful of air. Blinked away the moisture pooling beneath his eyelids. Tried to stop shaking.

"Nathan? Are you there?"

"Yeah." His ragged response was a mere whisper, more breath than word.

"I'm sorry you had to go through this. Danielle Price is the one who ought to be locked up." There was steel in J.C.'s voice, and leashed anger nipped at his words.

"What happened?"

"When I got back to the station, I met with the other detectives and gave them my take on the situation. One of the guys, a former NYPD cop, took the bracelet and went out to the Price house to do a little digging. Luckily, the woman's husband was just getting back from a fishing excursion. He didn't even know she'd called the police about the alleged theft. And he wasn't happy about it. My colleague had a ringside seat to the little domestic fracas that followed."

"What do you mean?"

"Turns out your client pulled this stunt once

before. With a gardener at their mainland home. So, faced with her husband's ire—and the potential loss of her sugar daddy—she backpedaled faster than a crook caught with the goods. She changed her story and said she had forgotten she was wearing the bracelet while you were there. Claims it has a faulty catch and that it must have fallen into the box when she handed you a tool."

"That's pretty lame."

"Tell me about it. And according to my colleague, her husband agreed, even though she tried every trick in the book to placate him. They were still battling it out when he left."

As relief surged through Nathan, his shaking intensified. He had to tighten his grip on the phone to keep it from slipping through his fingers. "Thanks, J.C."

"It didn't take much detective work to figure out her story stank as badly as a three-day-old flounder."

"Maybe not. But with my record, any other cop would have hauled me in first and asked questions later." The thought turned his stomach. Again. "If you hadn't been around…" His voice trailed off.

"That was a lucky break, no question about it."

"I think it was more than luck."

"You won't get any argument from me on that. So what are your plans for the rest of the day? You want to meet me for lunch? My treat."

Nathan didn't think his queasy stomach would welcome food any time in the near future.

"I appreciate the offer, J.C. But I think I'm going to go back to the cottage and chill for a while. If the weather clears later, I might head out to the beach and paint."

"Sounds like a plan. And listen, Nathan…don't let this get you down. One vindictive woman isn't worth losing sleep over. You've got a good future ahead of you. Put this incident behind you and move on."

"Yeah." *Easier said than done*.

"Call me if you need anything, okay?"

"I will. Thanks again."

As Nathan pocketed his phone, a ray of sun managed to break through the clouds in the distance, suggesting Mother Nature might redeem herself by salvaging what was left of this holiday weekend Friday.

The shaft of light, which imbued the newly cleansed world with a golden glow, dovetailed nicely with the favorable turn of events in his life, Nathan reflected. His name had been cleared. J.C. had come through for him again. He might even be able to get in a little painting today after all.

Only one thing was missing from that happy picture.

Catherine's faith in him.

And that cast a pall over the otherwise good news brightening his day.

Deciding to wait out the storm—and determined to focus on the positives—Nathan once more entered the quiet church and slid into a pew near the rear. This day could have turned out very differently, he knew. But for his brother's trust in him, he might very well be behind bars right now.

A shudder ran through.

"Thank you, Lord." He whispered the words, focusing on the cross in the sanctuary that symbolized the selfless love that had redeemed a world. That represented a man betrayed, who nevertheless continued to love—and forgive.

Give me compassion, too, Lord, Nathan prayed in silence. *Grant me empathy and understanding for Catherine, whose past has colored her perceptions. Please heal the ache in the part of my heart she awakened...and claimed as her own. Help me get past my hurt. And if there's a way to salvage the relationship we were starting to build, please open my heart to Your guidance so that I don't miss out on the chance of a lifetime.*

"Eat your lunch, Zach."

Picking up the cooling grilled-cheese sandwich on the plate in front of him, Zach played with the crust. "I'm not hungry."

She wasn't, either. Nevertheless, Catherine took a sip of her tepid soup. If it hadn't been for Zach, she would have skipped lunch altogether. But her son needed to eat.

"Come on…try a few bites."

He tore off a piece of crust. Crumbled it between his fingers. "Are you sure Nathan isn't going to come back later, for our party?"

Yes, she was sure. She'd seen the look of betrayal in his eyes when he'd detected her doubt. In that brief meeting of gazes, she'd failed him—and perhaps irreparably hurt their budding romance. Love required absolute trust, and she hadn't given him that. Far from it.

And after everything they'd shared, he'd deserved better from her.

The problem was, she didn't know how to repair the damage. A simple *I'm sorry* just didn't cut it.

"Mom?"

At Zach's prompt, she rose and carried her bowl of soup to the counter. "No, honey, he's not coming back today."

Or maybe ever.

Her heart plummeted at that very real possibility.

"Is he mad at us?"

She'd been fielding her son's litany of questions ever since Nathan pedaled away two hours ago. But none of her answers had satisfied him.

Nor had they satisfied her.

"No, Zach, he's not mad at us. He just had some things to think about."

She sat back down at the table and took his hand in hers, recalling how she'd marveled over every one of his perfect fingers the first time she'd held him in her arms. How she'd felt on top of the world. Invincible. Filled with joy—and confident about the future for her and David and their new son.

As she'd discovered, however, there were few perfect moments like that one. Mostly, life was a series of challenges. Of accepting imperfections and mistakes, adjusting to losses, overcoming obstacles. Of keeping the flame of hope alive even on the darkest days.

She hadn't always done a good job with any of those things. Not half as good as Nathan had. Despite horrendous odds, he'd turned his life around and become the kind of person others admire and try to emulate. A role model.

The kind of man any woman could love.

Yet she'd let old prejudices rear their ugly heads and jeopardize their future.

What a fool she'd been.

When the silence lengthened, Zach shoved back his chair and circled the table to climb into her lap. He didn't do that much anymore. Only when he was feeling scared or lonesome or confused.

All the things she, too, was experiencing at the moment.

She wrapped her arms around him, inhaling the comforting little-boy scent that always helped stabilize her world, and pulled him close.

Resting his cheek against her chest, he spoke in a quivery voice. "I have a feeling Nathan's never going to come back, Mom."

She had the same feeling. But she couldn't tell that to Zach. Not today. Not yet.

"He might."

"Maybe if you asked him to, he would."

Would he? she wondered. But what words could mitigate the damage she'd done, the pain she'd inflicted?

"Could you try, Mom?"

"I don't know what I would say, honey."

"Just tell him we really like him. And it's lonesome here without him. Tell him it feels like a rainy day even when the sun is shining."

That about summed it up, Catherine concluded.

Yet there was one more thing she could add.

She could also tell him she was falling in love with him. Maybe that admission would convince him to forgive her fleeting lack of faith in him.

Maybe.

"I'll think about it, Zach. Are you finished with your lunch?"

"Yeah."

The grilled-cheese sandwich lay almost untouched on his plate. Usually, she'd insist he eat at least a few bites. Today, she let it pass.

"Okay. Let's get you settled."

Fifteen minutes later, after reading him a story, she headed back downstairs. She wasn't in the mood for housework, but she needed something mindless to do while she planned her strategy. And worried about what was happening to Nathan. The thought that some spiteful, vindictive woman might be able to put him back behind bars made her blood run cold.

She couldn't begin to imagine the torment he must be experiencing.

Wandering into the laundry room, she began sorting through the dirty clothes in the hamper, her attention only half on her job. But when the Atlanta Braves jersey caught her eye, she froze. It still rested atop the dryer. Still unwashed. Still imbued with Nathan's scent.

She started to reach for it, but a small white triangle sticking out from between the washer and dryer distracted her. She bent to investigate—only to discover it was a white envelope. Containing her cash from the ATM.

As a stomach-clenching wave of regret washed over her, the pieces of her memory clicked into place.

She'd come in here yesterday after arriving home from her errands, lugging two boxes of laundry detergent. As she'd set them down, her purse had slipped off her shoulder. Irritated, she'd plopped it on top of the washer. Much to her annoyance, it had tipped over, spewing the contents over the surface just as Zach, in his eagerness to help, had dropped a bag of potatoes on the kitchen floor behind her.

The envelope must have fallen out and slipped between the two machines as she turned toward him.

Sick at heart, Catherine closed her eyes and drew a deep breath.

How could you be so dumb? And how could you have harbored even one millisecond of doubt about Nathan?

Her only excuse—and it wasn't sufficient, as she well knew—was that the baggage from her past was formidable. She was working through it, and had begun to accept that rehabilitation was possible for criminals, but she supposed enough skepticism had remained to raise a fleeting doubt after the money had gone missing. And that same doubt had flickered through her mind again when Zach had produced the bracelet from Nathan's tool kit.

Deep inside, though, she'd always known that

the kind, gentle man who had befriended her son and eroded the walls around her heart hadn't taken her money. Nor had he stolen the bracelet. No matter what that Price woman said.

The question was, could she convince him she believed in him? Or was it too late?

Catherine didn't know the answers to those questions. But she did know one thing.

He deserved her trust. And she intended to do everything she could to convince him he had it.

For always.

Chapter Fourteen

Nathan dipped his brush into the cobalt-blue paint he'd squeezed onto his palette, swirled it in the magenta, dabbed it in white and proceeded to do his best to replicate the amazing hue of the sea off Great Point.

This was his first visit to the isolated northern tip of the island, where a stately lighthouse dominated the evocative, windswept landscape. And it was exactly the kind of spot he'd been looking for when he'd asked Edith to recommend an area as far removed as possible from the Fourth of July weekend holiday crowds.

Getting here hadn't been easy, however. Edith had warned him to let some air out of the tires on J.C.'s car before attempting the sand road that led to the lighthouse, and he'd have to refill them at the air pump near the main road when he left. But this glorious stretch of beach was well worth the effort required to reach it. Although there was a small cluster of people close to the lighthouse, he'd trekked down quite a distance. As a result, he had a long stretch of untouched sand all to himself.

It was a good place to think. And regroup.

His top two priorities after the traumatic events of the morning.

Leaning forward on his portable stool, he concentrated on getting the curl of a wave just right. Then he turned his attention to the lighthouse, adding the outline of it to the scene on the canvas with bold, decisive strokes.

All the while wishing he had as much confidence in his future as he did in his painting skills.

When he'd come to Nantucket at J.C.'s and Marci's invitation, he hadn't had a long-term blueprint for his life. He'd planned to use their generous gift of three months in Edith's cottage to decompress, pick up some odd jobs and save enough money to give him a little cushion for whatever he decided to do once this interlude was over.

He definitely hadn't planned to fall in love.

But it seemed God had had other ideas.

Not that he was ready to commit to a serious step like marriage. If he'd learned one thing from his past, it was to move slowly. Analyze options. Make no rash decisions.

He had, however, been ready to explore the attraction between him and Catherine. Take it to the next level.

Until he'd seen the doubt in her eyes this morning.

And that, in turn, had made him think about a couple of troubling issues he hadn't factored into their relationship—but should have.

Like, how would being involved with an ex-con impact Catherine and Zach? Would the stigma he'd carry for the rest of his life taint them? Limit their opportunities? Undermine their reputations?

Tough questions.

But there was a tougher one.

Would he want people he loved to have to live with the risk that had been slammed home to him today as hard as a punch to the solar plexus—and which had left him just as breathless?

The harsh truth was that without J.C. to vouch for him, he would have been toast this morning. Back behind bars faster than the sand crabs on this beach were scuttling for their holes.

Was it fair to subject a family to the possibility that someone with an agenda could destroy their future? For the sake of Catherine and Zach, wasn't it better to break the relationship off now, anyway? Before things got too serious?

Because in the end, he cared too much to run the

risk of adding any more pain or loss to the lives of a woman and little boy who had already endured more than their share of both.

Even if walking away left his own life empty.

Shoving that depressing thought aside, Nathan forced himself to concentrate on transferring to canvas the evocative majesty of the lighthouse in front of him. He needed to clear his mind, give his dilemma to God and wait for guidance. It would come. It always did.

As he worked, focused on the task at hand, he didn't notice at first that a solitary figure had broken away from the small cluster of cars and people at the tip of the point and was moving his direction. When he did become aware of the intruder's approach, he stifled his disappointment. He didn't own the beach, after all. But he wasn't up to conversation. He hoped the lone walker would simply pass him by, not stop to chat as people often did while he was painting.

Doing his best to ignore the interloper—a strategy he hoped would send a clear *Keep Out* message—he didn't flick another discreet glance toward him or her until the person was fifty yards away.

That's when he realized it was a woman. One he knew very well.

His heart stuttered.

As Catherine drew closer, his hand began to tremble. Setting his brush down, he shaded his eyes and tried to breathe. She was dressed as she'd been this morning, in a floral-print skirt that billowed around her legs and a soft-lavender knit top that hinted at her curves. Her clunky hiking boots were in direct contrast to her feminine attire, but despite the reinforced footwear she seemed to be treading cautiously on the shifting sand beneath her feet. A towel was draped over her arm, and she was toting a small insulated container.

She stopped about six feet away from him and tucked her hair behind her ear. "Hi."

Her greeting was shy. Tentative. As if she was uncertain of her welcome.

"Hi." He wiped his hands on a rag and stood. "I didn't expect to see you again today."

"I'm not surprised."

When she didn't offer anything else, he asked the obvious question. "What are you doing way out here?"

"Looking for you."

He frowned. "How did you know where I was?"

"I stopped by your cottage. Edith told me."

Who else? His neighbor was the only who'd been privy to his destination. "Where's Zach?"

"Edith volunteered to watch him for a couple of hours."

Nathan arched an eyebrow. That was a first. "I'm surprised you left him with someone else."

She shrugged. "With school starting in seven weeks, I decided I'd better get used to it. And it wasn't a hard sell from his standpoint. There were two friendly little girls there, and Edith promised to make another batch of cinnamon rolls." She swallowed and moistened her lips, distracting him. "If I'm not bothering you, I'd like to talk for a few minutes."

His gaze shifted from her lips to her eyes. "You've always bothered me, Catherine. In a good way."

At his husky, honest response, soft color flooded her cheeks. "Can we sit for a few minutes? Edith gave me a beach towel. And she dug some cookies out of her freezer in case we got hungry. I think she also threw in a couple of sodas." She lifted the small insulated pack.

"Okay."

Moving closer, he took the tote and set it on the sand. Together they spread out the towel, then sat next to each other, facing the sea.

Nathan was tempted to take her hand. But he didn't. For all he knew, she'd sought him out to do no more than apologize. He knew she'd seen the hurt in his eyes this morning when doubt had flashed through her own. Perhaps she was simply sorry for causing him distress—and had no interest in taking their relationship any further.

Besides, he now had his own reservations about that, anyway. The last thing he wanted to do was hurt the woman and little boy who'd added such light and grace to his days. And the stigma from his past that would follow him for the rest of his life could do that.

He watched as she lifted a handful of sand and let it sift back to the beach. Some of the grains clung to her fingers despite several attempts to brush them off, and she tipped her head and studied them.

"You know, this is a good analogy for what's been happening to me in the past twenty-four hours." She extended her hand toward him and wiggled her fingers.

Her pensive voice was muffled by the boom of the waves, and he had to lean close to hear her. "How so?"

"I have a lot of baggage, Nathan, as you know. Meeting you forced me to take a hard look at a lot of it. And to accept the fact that people who have done bad things can change. Letting go of my views on that score has been tough for me. But I thought I'd managed it. Until my money went missing and Zach found the bracelet in your toolbox."

She made another attempt to brush off the grains still stuck to her fingers, yet some remained. "Like this sand, I discovered some of my prejudices were still clinging to me. But since you left, I did a lot of soul-searching. And I purged them from my heart."

Lacing her fingers in her lap, her expression grew earnest. "Here's the thing, Nathan. I can't take back that moment of doubt. I wish I could. But I can promise you it's gone forever. With every fiber of my being, I know you could no more steal money or a bracelet than I could neglect Zach. I can't tell you how sorry I am for my brief lapse of faith in you. All I can do is try my best to make up for it in the future—if you think we still might have one. And if you can dig deep in your heart and find a way to forgive me."

Catherine's earnest apology rekindled the tiny ember of hope buried beneath the ashes in his heart. Looking into her emerald eyes, mere inches from his, he saw nothing but sincerity.

And love.

Which made it all the more difficult to pull back. But he had to do that for the same reason she'd moved forward.

Love.

"The forgiveness part is easy, Catherine." He took one of her hands, brushed off the last of the clinging grains, and twined his fingers with hers. "But your lapse, as you called it, forced me do some hard thinking. I care for you and Zach. A lot. And I was beginning to think we had a future, too. But after all that's happened, I realized that by associating with me, you and Zach would be tainted by my mistakes. People could shun you. That wouldn't be fair to either of you."

A spark of anger flared to life in the depth of her green eyes. "If people can't judge you for who you are now, then I don't care what they think of me. And I wouldn't want to associate with those kind of people, anyway."

While her loyal words heartened him, there was more. "There's a risk, too, Catherine. I learned that today. If J.C. hadn't stood up for me, I would have been back behind bars. And no matter how hard I try to keep my nose clean, if I cross paths with the wrong kind of person, it could happen again. In a suspicious situation, my record will always work against me."

Her nostrils flared, and her eyes narrowed. "I don't think there are many people around as vindictive as the customer you had the misfortune to run into. I'm not worried about that, Nathan. And as for Danielle Price—we're not going to back off from this fight. I doubt your brother will let you, and I don't intend to, either."

We.

The word echoed like the peal of joyous bells in his mind. And told him two things. She considered them a team. And she didn't know he'd been cleared. But of course, she wouldn't. Who would have told her?

Meaning she'd come out here today believing in him despite Danielle's accusation. Despite that brief flicker of doubt in her eyes as they'd stood in front of her house.

As he tried to grasp the significance of that, she angled toward him and took his other hand. "Earlier today, as I was trying to figure out how to make amends, Zach gave me some good advice. He said, 'Just tell him we really like him. And it's lonesome here without him. Tell him it feels like a rainy day even when the sun is shining.' I can't improve on his language. So if you're willing to give this another go, I'd like to see where things might lead between us. Because the truth is, I…I think I'm falling in love with you. What do you say?"

The ember of hope in his heart burst into a flame that burned steady and strong. He wasn't certain what the future might hold for the two of them. But all at once he *was* certain he couldn't pass up the opportunity for happiness the Lord had sent his way. Whatever challenges their tomorrows might hold, Catherine's earnest speech and the warmth and determination in her eyes convinced him she was willing—and able—to meet them. As long as he stood by her side.

Which was exactly where he wanted to be.

"I say yes."

The tension in her features eased, and a slow smile lifted her lips as she leaned toward him. "Do you think we could put some action behind those words?"

Nathan didn't need any further encouragement. He leaned in, too—in time to hear a loud rumble from the vicinity of her stomach.

Flushing with embarrassment, she dipped her head and laid a hand on her abdomen. "Talk about ruining a romantic moment."

He chuckled. "I'm a little hungry myself. I skipped lunch." In truth, his appetite had returned with a vengeance.

"I only had a few spoonfuls of soup."

"How about we dip into Edith's cookies first? Feed the body before we feed the soul?"

She smiled and picked up the small insulated container. "Okay by me."

Setting it on her lap, she unzipped the top and withdrew two sodas. After passing one to Nathan, she pulled out a plastic bag of cookies. As she examined them, the soft blush retuned to her cheeks.

"What?" He leaned closer for a better look.

"She said she'd been saving these for a special occasion…" Catherine's words trailed off and she tipped the bag his way.

Edith had packed them heart-shaped short-bread cookies.

He burst out laughing. "The Lighthouse Lane matchmaker strikes again."

Catherine gave him a puzzled look. "What are you talking about?"

"Over the past few years, Edith has built quite a reputation as a matchmaker. And she's had us in her sights for weeks."

"You're kidding."

"Nope. And so far she's batting a thousand." He took the packet, pulled a cookie out for each of them and lifted his soda can in salute. "To Edith."

She clinked her can with his, and in short order they'd each demolished three cookies.

When he reached for cookie number four, she smiled. "You might want to save room for some cake. That is, if you still want to have that wrap party. A two-layer chocolate fudge supreme is waiting. And so is Zach."

He withdrew his hand. "I wouldn't miss it."

"Are we on for fireworks tomorrow night, too?"

The wind tossed some strands of hair across her face, and he lifted his hand to brush them aside, fingering their silky softness. Then he took her soda can and set it in the sand.

"I'll be there. But how about a little preview right now?"

The warmth in her eyes melted his heart. As did her whispered response: "I think that's a great idea."

As the surf crashed and the gulls circled overhead, Nathan reached over and gathered her into his arms, finding it hard to believe that this moment wasn't some fairy tale or a figment of his imagination. For happy endings had never been his lot in life.

But when Catherine's hands went around his neck, when he heard her soft sigh, when he felt the warmth of her breath on his cheek, when he inhaled the sweet scent of her skin…he finally believed it was real.

And as he claimed her sweet lips in a tender kiss filled with promise and possibilities, he knew that here, on this tiny speck of land in the Atlantic Ocean—a world away from the life he'd left behind—he would find the bright and shining tomorrow of his dreams.

Epilogue

Seven months later

"Watch your step. We don't want any more broken toes."

As Nathan smiled and extended his hand, Catherine took it and stepped out of the car in front of Sheltering Shores Inn.

Home.

Warm, welcoming light spilled from the windows of the main house, and a heart-shaped cranberry wreath hung on the front door. As she tucked her arm in Nathan's for the short walk past the banks of snow to the porch, she tipped her head back and inhaled a lungful of the cleansing, sea-kissed air. Above her, the night sky was crystal clear and studded with twinkling stars.

"What a perfect end to a perfect Valentine's Day," she murmured, her lips curving into a contented smile.

Nathan pulled her closer, his breath creating frosty clouds in the still night air as he spoke. "It's not over yet. I'm assuming you expect me to stick around for a while after we relieve Edith and Chester of babysitting duty."

She snuggled next to him. "That was my plan."

"Good." He leaned down to brush his lips across her forehead, then pulled back. "Wow! Your face is freezing!"

"But your lips are warm. How about warming mine up once we get inside?"

He chuckled. "That was *my* plan."

As they ascended the steps and Catherine started to reach into her purse for her keys, the front door opened.

"I thought I heard a car drive up." Edith, attired in white pants and a sparkly red sweater for the occasion, beamed at them. "Come in, come in. It's too cold to linger outside."

With Nathan's hand in the small of her back, Catherine moved past Edith and into the foyer. As she shrugged out of her coat, she glanced into the living room. A fire was burning in the grate, soft music was playing and at least a dozen candles were adding a warm glow to the room.

She smiled up at Nathan as he took her coat, and his wink told her he'd noticed the romantic ambiance, too.

The matchmaker was still at work.

But Cathcrine didn't mind in the least. And she was very grateful Edith had volunteered to babysit tonight. She and Zach and Nathan could have had dinner together here at the inn, as they had on many previous special occasions. But Nathan had insisted on a first-class Valentine's Day celebration after all the years he'd spent the holiday alone, in a cell.

Catherine hadn't argued. She'd wanted a night to remember, too.

So far, it was exceeding her expectations. He'd arrived with two dozen long-stemmed red roses. Plied her with designer chocolates. Treated her to an elegant gourmet dinner in town. And now a candlelit room awaited them.

"Here you go, Edith." Chester appeared from the back of the house, toting Edith's coat. His own was already on.

"You don't have to rush out," Catherine protested.

"Of course we do. It's Valentine's Day. We have some billing and cooing of our own to do."

Chester's cheeks flushed crimson as he helped Edith on with her coat.

"Zach went down an hour ago," Edith relayed, oblivious to her husband's embarrassment as she pulled on her gloves. "You two should have some nice quiet time together. And a cold night is always a good excuse to get cozy. Well, we're off." She tucked her arm in Chester's and propelled him across the foyer.

"Thanks again, Edith," Catherine called as the couple exited through the door, admitting a blast of icy air as they left.

"My pleasure. You two go take advantage of that nice fire."

The door shut behind them.

"Subtlety isn't her strong suit." Catherine gave Nathan a wry smile.

"No. But she has a heart of gold."

"True." Tipping her head, she regarded him. He had one shoulder propped against the doorway leading into the dining room and didn't appear to be in any hurry to remove his coat. "I thought you were staying awhile."

"I am. But I have to get a present from the car. I just want to give Edith and Chester a chance to get away before I go back out."

The warmth of his smile did more to chase away the evening chill than the fireplace ever could.

"You've already spent enough on me tonight, Nathan."

"You're worth it. And I can afford an occasional extravagance."

That was true. Over the past seven months, he'd sold a dozen paintings. All had commanded sizeable prices. And his reputation was growing. A gallery in Boston had already approached him about doing a show in the fall.

But his financial resources weren't the point.

"I already have the best gift." She moved close and took his hands. "You."

He dipped his head to claim a kiss, but as she reached up to put her arms around his neck, he backed off, holding her at arm's length.

"Now you behave, young woman, or we'll never get to the present."

She sidled closer, loving the way their relationship had evolved into a comfortable give and take, filled with teasing and laughter and a joy so complete her heart sometimes ached with the sweetness of it.

"I'll take the kiss instead."

"No, you won't. Trust me, you'll want this present. Now, go wait in the living room."

Heaving a put-upon sigh, she swiveled away, sending the skirt of her cranberry-red silk dress floating around her legs in a flirty flounce. "Hurry back."

Nathan turned up his collar and wiggled his eyebrows. "Count on it."

Grinning, she watched as he disappeared through the front door. Then she retrieved a red-foil-wrapped package from the kitchen and wandered over to the sofa. Thanks to Nathan, the rest of her home now looked as good as the two guest rooms that had been booked solid through the fall and were already being reserved for next season. He'd labored over it with the same meticulous care he gave to every task he undertook.

That's why she'd been able to recommend him without hesitation to several clients who had hired her to redecorate their homes. Not that he needed much of that kind of work these days. But he said it kept him grounded. And that it gave him a sense of security his painting didn't yet afford.

Settling into the cushions on the sofa, she decided she liked Edith's selection of music. Gershwin was always a good choice for romance.

The front door opened. Shut. She heard fabric sliding over fabric. The jangle of a coat hanger. And then Nathan joined her.

Empty handed.

She hefted the present in her lap. "I have yours. Where's mine?"

"In the hall. Why don't I open mine first?"

She smiled. "Anxious, aren't we?"

"Presents are still a novelty for me."

Although his tone was light, her throat tightened. They didn't talk much about his dark days anymore. Or the childhood that had been stolen from him. But at unexpected moments, she sometimes caught a fleeting, shadowed glimpse of the innocent little boy he'd never had a chance to be.

She handed over the package without another word.

Tearing off the paper, he pulled out a glossy art book featuring the work of the classic Impressionist painters he admired.

"This is fabulous, Catherine." He flipped through it, devouring the images as hungrily as the birds searched for seeds in the feeder outside her kitchen window on a cold winter day. "I can't wait to give this my full attention." After checking out a few more pages, he set it aside and shifted toward her. "But for now, I plan to give *you* my full attention."

At the undercurrent of excitement in his voice, her pulse accelerated.

"Wait here." Rising, he retreated to the foyer. Half a minute later, he returned carrying a large, flat package wrapped in silver paper and tied with a large red bow. He sat beside her and passed it over in silence.

She could tell as he set it in her lap that it was a frame. With great care, she pulled off the paper—and as she gazed at the beautifully executed painting inside, her breath caught in her throat.

It was a portrait of her and Zach at the beach. But unlike the piece she'd seen at Blue Water Gallery, this one was filled with joy and love and optimism.

The two of them were standing barefoot at the edge of the water. Zach wore shorts and a T-shirt, and he was squatting down, preparing to dig a half-submerged shell out of the wet sand with a stick. She had on the floral print skirt and lavender knit top she'd worn at Great Point the day they'd shared Edith's heart-shaped cookies, and she was brushing aside a few flyaway strands of hair with one hand. Her other hand hovered over Zach, as if she'd just let him go, her fingers still extended toward her son. Close enough to help him if he needed her, but far enough way to give him room to explore on his own.

Catherine was blown away.

Through a subtle use of body language, Nathan had captured the dilemma she continued to struggle with—how to give Zach space to breathe and grow yet still protect him.

But beyond that, he'd also portrayed her as a woman in love, her eyes joy-filled, her expression reflecting utter contentment and peace. The emotions Nathan had imbued her with in this painting were exactly the ones she'd felt since he'd come into her life.

It was masterful.

Angling toward him, she blinked away the sudden moisture that blurred her vision. "This is wonderful, Nathan. I can't think of a better Valentine's Day present."

"I hope it's more than that."

The husky timbre of his voice and the soft light in his eyes played havoc with her respiration. "What do you mean?"

He reached into his jacket pocket and withdrew a small jeweler's box.

She stopped breathing.

"This goes with it. I hope." Flipping open the top, he revealed a huge diamond solitaire on a gold band.

Catherine gasped.

"Oh, my word…" She stared at the gorgeous ring, awed by its message, its beauty—and a price tag she couldn't even begin to fathom. "Nathan…it's too much. I know you're doing well, but this is way too extravagant. You don't need to ply me with diamonds to convince me to…"

He pressed his fingers to her lips. "Catherine. I bought this with the money from my second painting."

The one of the little boy in the storm she'd surreptitiously viewed at Blue Water Gallery.

Her protest died in her throat.

Nathan knew she'd seen it. She'd finally told him about her impromptu visit, a few weeks after he'd shared the story of his childhood trauma. How fitting that the profit from that painting, which had been inspired by the pain and darkness of his old life, would fund a symbol that represented a new and shining future.

She gave a slow nod of understanding as love and admiration for this special man overflowed in her heart. "That's a good use for that money."

"I thought you'd understand." He removed the ring from the box, and when he took her hand she felt the tremors in his fingers. "So I'm hoping the painting can do double duty—as both a valentine and an engagement present."

"What's an engagement?"

At the question from the foyer, they turned in unison. Zach was standing on the threshold of the living room, trailing a blanket behind him, rubbing his eyes and stifling a yawn.

Clasping Nathan's free hand, Catherine found her voice first. "It's a promise to get married, honey."

On cue, Nathan dropped to one knee beside her and grinned at Zach. "That's exactly what it is, champ. And now I'm going to show you how a man is supposed to propose."

When he looked at her, his eyes were filled with a love so deep and abiding and tender that she, too, started to tremble.

"Catherine Walker, I love you with every fiber of my being. When I came to Nantucket to start a new life, I never expected to find love, as well. But God, in His infinite wisdom and generosity, gave me the greatest blessing of my life when He set me in your path. And I want to walk that path with you for all the days He grants us. So…" He swallowed. Took a deep breath. "Will you please do me the honor of becoming my wife?"

She smiled through her tears and opened her mouth to respond. But Zach beat her to it.

"Yes!" His joyous shout echoed through the house, and he bounded over to stand behind the couch. "You did that really good, Nathan."

Nathan grinned. "Thanks, champ." He turned to Catherine, and his eyes searched hers. Hopeful. Tender. And—endearingly—just the slightest bit uncertain. "Your turn."

She wasted no time putting his mind at ease. Leaning close, she draped her arms around his neck and gave him a teary smile. "I defer to my son's very sound judgment. My answer is yes, too."

Joy flooded his face, and he slipped the ring on her finger, then pulled her close for a chaste kiss.

"That's to seal the deal," he murmured against her lips. "I promise to do better later."

"I'll hold you to that," she whispered back.

"This is so cool!" Zach scampered around the couch and flung himself at the two of them.

As they accepted Zach's exuberant hugs and pulled him into the circle of their embrace, their gazes met over his head. And all at once, as she basked in the warmth of Nathan's smile, Catherine was struck by the irony of their happily-ever-after. For the past two years, since tragedy had destroyed her world, she'd lived with hate and fear, in a prison of her own making. Yet a man who'd spent ten years behind bars had set her free.

For with his courage and kindness and love, Nathan had shown her how to create her own tomorrow. And by example, he'd helped her rediscover the centering power of faith. To let hate and anger go. To love without smothering. And to trust once again.

Catherine knew that not all of their tomorrows would be smooth. But with Nathan by her side, she was confident they'd triumph over every challenge. Because no power on earth was stronger than love.

As if reading her mind, Nathan tugged Zach

close with one arm and pulled her near with the other.

"This is what I always wanted," he said against her hair, his voice choked with emotion.

"Yeah. Now we can be a real family," Zach piped up. "Isn't this great?"

Indeed it was, Catherine reflected, listening to the steady, comforting beat of Nathan's heart beneath her ear. And wrapping her arms around the two people who were the center of her world, she gave thanks. For the healing power of love. For a tomorrow filled with hope. For a son who was blossoming. And for the man from Lighthouse Lane, whose caring heart and grace-filled soul had transformed her life.

Now and forever.

* * * * *

Dear Reader,

Welcome back to LIGHTHOUSE LANE!

When I began this series, I only planned to write three books. But after meeting the Clay family, I knew I couldn't leave Nantucket without telling Nathan's story.

Starting over is tough anytime, but for an ex-con it's especially hard. Fortunately, he had a brother and sister who loved him—and a faith that sustained him. But then he had to go and fall in love with a woman who held men with a criminal past in special disdain. Overcoming that hurdle proved to be one of the biggest challenges of his life. Yet along the way, both he and Catherine brought out the best in each other. And isn't that what love is all about?

I hope you enjoyed the journey to LIGHTHOUSE LANE as much as I did. And please watch for new books from me in the future. Because there's always another good story waiting to be told!

QUESTIONS FOR DISCUSSION

1. As an ex-con, Nathan fears he will carry a stigma that will affect the rest of his life. Do you think this is true? Why or why not?

2. When the book begins, Catherine harbors deep hate for the man who killed her husband. And she doesn't believe criminals can be rehabilitated. What happens in the course of the story to change her mind? Cite specific instances.

3. Because Catherine lost the man she loved in a violent crime that took place practically in her backyard, she's terrified of losing Zach. As a result, she overprotects him. Have you ever done this, or witnessed it in others? What is the potential negative impact on the child?

4. Zach overreacts to the spaghetti sauce on Nathan's shirt. Few children go through what Zach did, yet many less traumatic (but unsettling) events have long-term implications for youngsters. Name some situations (one-time or ongoing) that might have a negative influence on a child. How might that influence be manifested immediately—or later in life?

5. Catherine turned away from God after her husband was killed. Discuss the reasons why. Have you ever felt alienated from the Lord? Why? How did you reconnect?

6. What compels Nathan to share his darkest secret with Catherine? Does it affect their relationship? How?

7. When Catherine's money disappears, she tries to squelch her suspicions of Nathan. But when another customer accuses him of stealing her bracelet, those suspicions return. Did this surprise you? How do you think you would have reacted in this situation?

8. Nathan sees the doubt in Catherine's eyes after he's accused of stealing and is disheartened. Why is trust so vital to a relationship?

9. Catherine finds solace in her music, just as Nathan finds it in his painting. Why do creative endeavors often allow us to express our deepest emotions safely? What do you turn to when you need a release valve? Or when you want to enrich your life in a joyful way?

10. Nathan has a very close relationship with his brother and sister. How do you think those

connections helped him get through his final years in prison? Do you have a close relationship with your siblings? Why or why not? If not, what actions might you take to strengthen those ties?

11. Because of Nathan's record, Danielle's accusation is particularly dangerous. Without J.C. to run interference for him, Nathan could have ended up back behind bars. Have you ever run into someone who was truly vindictive? How did you deal with it? Did it have any long-term repercussions? What does Scripture tell us about this?

12. Nathan has a very checkered past. He admits he's done bad things. Yet he's made his peace with his mistakes and moved on. How does a strong relationship with the Lord allow us to do that? Talk about how we can apply His example of forgiveness to our own lives. Is there someone you need to forgive? What is holding you back? What guidance does Scripture offer?

13. At the end of the book, Nathan gives Catherine a perfect Valentine's Day—complete with a proposal! What was your most memorable Valentine's Day? What made it so special?

One step into the living room and she froze again, pan aloft.

A hulking shape stood in shadow just inside the French doors leading out to the garden veranda. This was not Popbottle Jones. This was a big, bulky, dangerous-looking man. She raised the pan higher.

"What do you want?"

"Annie?" He stepped into the light.

All the blood drained from Annie's face. Her mouth went as dry as saltines. "Sloan Hawkins?"

The man removed a pair of silver aviator sunglasses and hung them on the neck of his black rock-and-roll T-shirt. He'd rolled the sleeves up, baring muscular biceps. A pair of eyes too blue to define narrowed, looking her over as though he were a wolf and she a bunny rabbit.

Annie suppressed an annoying shiver.

It was Sloan, all right, though older and with more muscle. His nearly black hair was shorter now—no more bad-boy curl over the forehead—but bad boy screamed off him in waves just the same. He was devastatingly handsome, in a tough, rugged, manly kind of way. The years had been kind to Sloan Hawkins.

She really wanted to hate him, but she'd already wasted too much emotion on this outlaw. With God's help, she'd learned to forgive. But she wasn't about to forget.

*Will Sloan and Annie's faith be strong
enough to see them through
the pain of the past and allow them to open
their hearts to a possible future?
Find out in THE WEDDING GARDEN
by Linda Goodnight,
available May 2010 from Love Inspired.*